DRAUGR

DRAUGR

by Arthur G. Slade

ORCA BOOK PUBLISHERS

Canadian Cataloguing in Publication Data
Slade, Arthur G. (Arthur Gregory)
Draugr

ISBN 1-55143-094-0
I. Title. II. Series: Northern frights (Victoria, BC)
PS8587.L343D72 1997   jC813'.54   C97-910423-8
PZ7.S628835Dr 1997

Library of Congress Catalog Card Number: 97-68869

Orca Book Publishers gratefully acknowledges the support of our publishing
programs provided by the following agencies: the Department of Canadian
Heritage, the Canada Council for the Arts, and the British Columbia Ministry
of Small Business, Tourism and Culture.

Cover design by Christine Toller
Cover illustration and interior illustrations by Ljuba Levstek

Printed and bound in Canada

Orca Book Publishers   Orca Book Publishers
PO Box 5626, Station B   PO Box 468
Victoria, BC V8R 6S4   Custer, WA 98240-0468
Canada   USA

97 98 99   5 4 3 2 1

This novel is dedicated with love to my parents Robert and Anne Slade. I owe you so much more than I can ever repay.

I also want to extend my gratitude to Emily, the town librarian. Thanks for lifting those heavy books on Norse mythology and passing them down to me when I was a little boy.

And my apologies to the wonderful inhabitants of Gimli, Manitoba. In the course of writing this novel I may have accidentally moved around an ice cream shop, a graveyard, and a few other things. I promise to put them back when I'm done with them.

Draugr (draw-gur) *m.* 'undead' man, ghost

–   Definition taken from
     E.V. Gordon's *An Introduction to Old Norse*

» 1 «

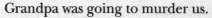Grandpa was going to murder us.

Not with an axe. Not with a shovel. But with words.

"Sarah sit down," Grandpa said softly to me. "I haven't even started my story."

"But I'm scared already." I'm young, I'm fourteen, and I have my limits. His last tale ended with a headless woman searching through the streets for her head every Halloween. I wasn't going to sleep tonight. Why did Mom and Dad send me here every summer?

Grandpa rubbed his big, rough hands together. He was tall and even though he was in his late seventies, he had the energy of a man half his age. "This is my last yarn for tonight. I promise. And it's my best one."

I sat down. At the bottom of my beating heart, I really did like his stories. So did Michael, my twin brother, and my cousin Angie, who were both hugging pillows, waiting for Grandpa to begin. Michael and I looked nearly the same, with blue eyes and dark hair. Except, of course, he was a boy and about half as smart as me. Angie was our opposite, with bright red hair and green eyes. This was one of the few times that she was actually quiet.

Grandpa smiled and his face creased into a thousand wrinkles. "The difference between this story and the others is this one is true. Every word of it. I do want to ask you a question before I begin though … are you afraid of death?"

"Well …" I started. "Uh … I haven't really thought about it."

"That's alright, Sarah," Grandpa said softly. In the dim light he looked suddenly older and tired, as if just voicing that question had taken years from his life. He cleared his throat. "I have an even more important thing to ask you. Are you afraid of the dead?"

How do you answer something like that? What do you say? "No," I lied. Michael and Angie shook their heads. This was becoming a little too weird, even for me.

Grandpa stared, those blue haunted eyes of his looking right through me. He seemed to be in a trance.

"Yoo hoo, Grandpa!" Michael called. He snapped his fingers. Once. Twice.

No reaction.

"Are you okay?" I whispered. "Grandpa?"

Grandpa shook his head. *"Draugr,"* he whispered as he crossed himself. The name echoed through the room and though I didn't know its meaning, I felt it. There in the quivering of my stomach, in the dryness of my throat. The name.

Grandpa was still staring. I whispered to him, but he didn't seem to hear me. Finally he looked directly into my eyes. "Long ago," he said, his voice even and controlled, "when I was quite young and I still lived in Iceland, I had an evil cousin, evil in the way only men can be evil. He respected no one, not his parents, not his kinsmen. No one. He complained about the work he had to do, about the way others did their work. He had venom in his blood and his tongue was like a serpent's — he spit only insults at the world and defied everything. His name was Borth."

Grandpa paused. He closed his eyes and I imagined him looking back in time, seeing his cousin standing amidst snow-covered hills in Iceland.

Grandpa opened his eyes again, still staring into the distance. "Borth was a strong youth, he could outwrestle many of the men in the valley and he loved fighting. His mother died giving birth to him and from that day forward he carried *harmathr* — bad luck. If he walked by your house, your cows would run loose, your food would burn in the oven; women would prick their thumbs if he entered a room as they were sewing. He used to hit me as if I were nothing more than a bag of flour. No one had any love for Borth.

"One day in December I murdered him. Not by myself, I had help, but I *murdered* him. I know I am old and harmless now, but then I was beaten, a beast, a dog. I had been kicked by my cousin too often and finally a time came when I could take my revenge. A group of us, my kinsmen and friends who had all been violated in one way or another by Borth, made a pact to teach him a lesson. We were just children, that's all. Children, hardly even as old as you three. I was the eldest though, and they all followed me.

"We hid in the pass at Ogen's valley, all six or seven of us, on a night when there was a full moon. We knew Borth would cut through the valley on his way into the village. We had dressed in rags and made masks of wood and feathers, so that we looked like mound dwellers. Some of us had even caught snakes to throw at him. Just to scare Borth, that's all we wanted, to run around and poke him with sticks, to yell his name, and then run away. It was supposed to be a trick, a warning, nothing more.

"Borth rode up a little after dark. The clomping of his horse, a beast as huge and evil as him, echoed in our ears.

I glanced and saw that my companions were frozen with fright, hypnotized by that sound and the sight of Borth. He looked so big in the saddle, his shoulders as gigantic as a troll's, his long cloak flowing down behind him.

"I knew nobody would move unless I did, that we would sit there and he would pass. Our moment would pass. So right before he arrived, I threw myself onto the path in front of him and screamed, waving my arms and launching a handful of dirt. Everyone else followed me, yelling and hooting around the horse, slapping its legs with their sticks. We were like little dwarves up from out of the ground, finally getting our revenge. His mount reared up, its giant hooves sliced the air above us. It neighed in anger, nostrils flaring. But we weren't frightened; we felt strong then, all of us, powerful with vengeance. We continued our attacks. The horse reared again and Borth shouted in anger, yanking with all his strength on the reins. One rein snapped and he tumbled from the saddle, still yelling.

"The path was very rocky. Even above the ruckus we were making, I heard a soft thud when his head struck a stone. His horse bolted and we surrounded Borth, poking him with sticks and kicking at him, screaming his name in our lust for vengeance. Then as one, realizing something was wrong, we stopped. Borth didn't move. We all looked at each other, but no one said anything. We knew he was dead.

"I don't know who ran first, one of us did, and then we all followed, just running and running down the pass and across the fields, away from Borth's body.

"One of the villagers found him the next morning in a pool of frozen blood. We buried him three days later in the family cemetery. It was a strange funeral. No one cried. No one could.

"I returned to my daily work, not able to tell anyone my

story. And I prayed nobody would discover what we had done. Then one morning, about two weeks after his death, I went into my family's hen house and found one of our chickens dead on the floor. It had been strangled. There were no tooth marks, so I knew it hadn't been killed by an animal. I figured one of the children from the village was just playing games and I forgot about it. But when I came back the next morning, another chicken was dead. This time its legs and head had been severed and placed beside its body. It made me sick to see, sick and very angry that someone would do this to our livestock. So I decided to catch whoever it was.

"That night I took my pitchfork with me and I stayed in the coop. I leaned up against the far wall. The coop was small. I could almost reach the door from where I was standing. It was warm too and I was dressed in a thick coat, so I soon sat down in the hay on the floor and fell asleep. I dreamed of a river filled with acid and blood that was slowly overflowing its banks. There were snakes in that river, huge snakes, the sons of Jormungand. Fire burned along the far bank. It was a strange, powerful dream, a dream from the old times.

"Then a noise woke me. The hens were moving around restlessly in the same way they do on the day I take them to the block. I stood up, still tired, the dream making my thoughts slow. I could sense the same thing as the chickens. The feeling that Death was floating through the air, searching. I wanted to get in a corner, to hide, but there was nowhere to go. I waited.

"At first nothing happened, then I heard a noise like something being slowly dragged across the ground outside the coop. The sound would stop, then start again. There was this growling too. The noises ended before I could really be sure I heard them. I breathed in, relieved, then the door to the coop creaked inwards against the wooden bolt. A scratching sound filled my ears, as if a huge nail were being slowly drawn from the top of the door to the bottom. I froze, my breath caught in my mouth. The chickens had stopped moving. Everything was completely silent.

"Then again came the scratching, this time louder, harder, so it seemed a groove was being dug into the wood. The door began to rattle, the whole coop creaked as if a giant hand were pushing on its side. I felt suddenly cold. The scratching started for a third time; one of the planks on the door snapped, and splinters and wood fell in on me.

"I could wait no longer. I grabbed my pitchfork, stepped forward, and yanked the shaking door open. An icy wind swept straight into my eyes and I had to squint against it. Before me, with one arm raised, was a huge shadowy man, misshapen in the moonlight. He took a shambling step towards me and became clearer so that I saw he was covered with dirt. Grass was stuck in his frozen messy hair. He stepped again, moving as if his legs were made of wood. I realized his head was not frozen with water but with black blood. His eyes glowed.

" *'Cousin,'* he rasped. He stepped again. *'I hate you.'*

"A huge white hand reached towards me. I stepped back, slipped, and struck my head on the hen's loft. I fell unconscious to the floor. There I slept as if dead.

"When I awoke, hours later, I was sore and stiff and there was a dirty palm print on my jacket.

"I knew what had happened to Borth. He was a *draugr*, a revenant. My cousin was so full of hate he had become the walking dead. I did not know what I should do. The next time he returned he would drag me to his lair and tear me limb from limb. So I went home, took the silver cross my mother had given me, and I walked to the cemetery and buried that holy symbol in the soft dirt of his grave.

"He has not come back, but he is not gone. He waits underneath that earth. The dead know who killed them, they know, and if they hate enough — if they hate enough — they'll find a way back. Sometimes I can hear him screaming in the wind. And I wonder what will happen if someone goes to his grave and removes the cross?"

Grandpa leaned back in his chair. He looked very serious. Once or twice I caught him staring at the door as if he thought something might be lurking outside.

We sat there silently for a few minutes.

Grandpa clapped his hands, startling all of us. "Bed time," he said. "Hope you have a great sleep."

We slowly got up and prepared for bed. When I came out of the bathroom, most of the lights were off and Michael and Angie had gone to their rooms. Grandpa was sitting in his reading chair, squinting at an old book. A full moon shone through the window, giving him a pale, eerie look.

"Grandpa," I whispered, "how come the moon's so bright tonight?"

He looked up, seemed a little surprised to see me. "Oh," he said, "it's just a full moon — the *Hagalaz* moon. The kind of moon that makes hair grow on werewolves."

"*What?*"

He winked. "I'm kidding. It's just your everyday normal moon. Nighty-night."

I went to bed. It took me quite a while to fall asleep.

» 2 «

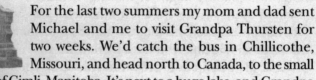For the last two summers my mom and dad sent Michael and me to visit Grandpa Thursten for two weeks. We'd catch the bus in Chillicothe, Missouri, and head north to Canada, to the small town of Gimli, Manitoba. It's next to a huge lake, and Grandpa lives in a six-room log cabin in the trees there.

Grandma Gunnora, his wife, used to live there too, but she died four years ago. I think that's one of the reasons Mom and Dad want us to come here — to keep Grandpa company. The other reason is they want to get us out of the house. We tend to get a little crazy when school's out.

This year Angie, my favorite cousin, was allowed to go with us and I was really looking forward to all the fun we'd have. Angie's not only my cousin, but she's one of my best friends too. I usually get to see her three or four times a year … but never for two weeks in a row.

It was our first morning at Grandpa's and the first full day of our vacation.

"Let's go for a walk," Angie suggested after we were finished breakfast. She was wearing a plaid shirt and had tied her red hair in a long ponytail. She'd been bouncing around the kitchen, putting away dishes and humming for the last ten minutes.

Like her whole family, Angie was a cheery morning person. I always found it a little revolting. She slid the last dish into the cupboard and rubbed her hands together, giving me a mischievous smile. "We might meet some of the locals. Maybe you'll finally find someone desperate enough to date you, Sarah."

"You take that back!" I demanded, but Angie just laughed and soon I couldn't help but chuckle too. She was right, I wasn't really lucky in the guy department. "I'll tell Grandpa."

I went into the living room where Grandpa was sitting with his cup of coffee in one hand and the same old book in the other. He hooked a finger around his reading glasses, slid them down his nose a little and looked up at me. "You're going to go for a walk. I know. I heard Miss Bright Eyes announce it to the world." He motioned me closer and asked quietly, "Does she have a volume knob?" I shook my head, laughing. Grandpa, like me, was definitely not a morning person. "Well," he shrugged, "it would be nice to have you kids out of my hair — I mean, have a pleasant walk. And don't fall down any holes. You might meet a rabbit you don't like."

He was always saying things like that. I'd probably find them funny if I could understand them.

Michael was out on the porch, sitting in Grandpa's rocking chair, catching the first warm rays of the sun. He looked like he was asleep.

Angie and I tried to tiptoe past, but the moment we got to the steps, he announced, "I'm coming too!"

We rolled our eyes and pretended to be upset.

"You two would get lost without me." Michael was grinning now, and walking towards us.

He's not my identical twin, by the way, but we do look quite a bit alike. The only difference is in our mouths. His tends to open up and tell stupid jokes constantly — I tend to be silent and tasteful.

But I will admit that Michael is my other best friend. We're the same age — we've been through so much together. Always in the same classrooms, hanging out with the same friends, playing on the same teams. I don't know what I would do without him.

We headed out of the yard. A few minutes later all three of us were walking north down the road, away from Grandpa's cabin. We soon came to the lake and decided to follow the shore, kicking at driftwood and passing by all the other cabins. I could hear a chainsaw growling in the distance and I imagined there were a lot of sleepy neighbors cursing that noise.

Not too many people were up yet. We went by a cabin where a middle-aged, sour-faced man stared at us like we were aliens. "Morning!" I said, waving, but he continued to glare. We hurried past. Were all the locals like this?

"I shoulda mooned him," Michael said when the cabin was out of sight. "That woulda given him something to stare at."

Angie laughed. "Or scared him back into his home, at least."

"Hey!" Michael gave her a friendly shove. "It's an honor to see my bare — "

"I don't want to hear this!" I interrupted. "There are some things I just don't want to picture."

Both Angie and Michael started chuckling. "Okay, okay," Michael said finally, "no more butt jokes for the rest of our holiday."

I sighed. We continued on, going past more cabins, some of them huge, with three levels and three-car garages. But the farther we went, the smaller and older the buildings seemed to get, until we passed two or three in a row with broken windows and lopsided doors and no sign of anyone living inside.

A few steps further and we found a group of cabins whose roofs had collapsed. There was a swampy smell surrounding them and it was darker here, as if the light couldn't quite reach this place. I was starting to feel a little edgy. It looked like this part of the lake had been abandoned

We kept walking. Soon we found ourselves away from the lake in a little clearing with a small stream. There were no footprints, paths, or signs of buildings. It was warm and muggy, even though the trees were now casting thick shadows across us. I heard frogs croaking up a storm, but they clammed up as we approached.

We wandered farther into the clearing. Feeling like a rest, Angie and I sat on a log and stretched our legs.

"I'm going to catch a Kermit." Michael rubbed his hands together. "Maybe we can have frog legs soup for lunch."

"Oh, gross," I said.

"I hear it tastes like chicken," Michael said over his shoulder and went wandering off.

"His brain gets smaller every day," Angie pointed out.

I laughed. "Yeah, sometimes it's hard to believe we're related."

Angie smiled.

I couldn't. Because I suddenly had this strong feeling that something was wrong here. That we were in danger.

A moment later Angie gave me a funny look. "You sick?" she asked. "How come your face is so pale?"

"I … I don't know," I said, looking around the clearing. Everything looked normal. "No reason, I guess."

A second later, Michael called out, "Hey, get off your butts and get over here. I found something cool."

"I'm kinda frightened to see what he thinks is cool,"

Angie whispered. She got up and started on the way to where Michael was standing. It took me a moment to stand, the effort left me exhausted. I had to struggle to catch up with Angie.

"It's a path," Michael announced when we got there.

"I can see that, Sherlock," Angie answered. She was bent over, tightening the laces on her boots. "The question is … where does it go to?"

"I don't know if we should … " I started. "… uh, guys."

They were already heading down the path. I followed. At first the trail was straight and easy, but within a few hundred yards it twisted around the hills and led deeper into the trees. I was pretty sure I could find my way back, but I wished I had a long spool of string to trail behind us like they did in all the fairy stories.

"I'm glad I brought my hiking boots," Angie said.

"Me too," I answered. My feet felt safe in the big, thick Hi-Techs. Like I could climb anything.

The trees became wider and taller so that they blocked out most of the light.

"We probably won't find any new friends here." Angie was looking around. I wondered if she was feeling the same uneasiness as me.

"HELLO, NEW FRIENDS!" I yelled, to show I wasn't frightened. Angie's back straightened and I realized I had startled her. She frowned at me. I shrugged. "I don't think there's a soul around. It doesn't seem like anyone's been out here for years."

Michael had jogged ahead and had almost disappeared around a corner. He certainly seemed to be in a hurry to go nowhere. Angie and I doubled our pace until we caught up with him.

Now the trees were definitely bigger and older, their

thick, dark roots creeping over the path. Twice I almost tripped. I was starting to get a little tired and hungry. I wondered how long we had been out here. I looked at my wrist but it was bare.

"What time is it?" I asked.

Both Michael and Angie stared at their empty wrists. They had forgotten their watches too.

Michael looked at his other wrist. "I swear I put mine on this morning. I remember taking it off the dresser next to the bed."

"I wonder if we should go back?" Angie whispered. She looked a little pale.

"Grandpa's probably getting worried about us," I added. "We've been gone for hours, I bet. It might even be lunch time."

Michael shook his head. His dark hair had flipped over one eye. "Let's just explore a little further. This has to go somewhere."

"Well … okay," I agreed. Angie nodded but didn't meet my eyes. We went ahead.

The path grew narrower and now the trees seemed to be leaning over us. We were in a world that was part shadows and part light. And it was cold. Some of the winter air still clung to these trees.

"I see something — someone," Michael said a second later. He was a few yards ahead of us again.

"What is it?" I strained my eyes.

"A little kid, I think."

We came over a rise and into a dimly lit clearing. Michael was right. There, standing next to a dying tree, was a young boy, maybe five years old. His clothes were ragged and torn. He was shimmering and hard to see.

"Go away," he moaned. *"Go away. Bad here."*

» 3 «

 "Do you think he's sick?" I asked. He certainly seemed unhealthy, all pale and thin. He leaned against the tree. His mouth was still moving, but no sounds were coming out now. We walked slowly towards him.

"It looks like there's something wrong with him … like he's lost," Angie said. "But how come we can't get near him?" The closer we came, the further away the boy seemed to get, moving from tree to tree. But he still stared at us, holding one hand out as a warning.

His mouth opened and closed. A second later I heard the words as if they were being carried on the wind. *"Go away!"*

We edged closer. He retreated backwards, but I couldn't see his feet move. He seemed to be drifting away from us.

"I'm going to run," Michael announced.

"I don't think that's — " I started to say, but Michael had already dashed off. He pushed branches aside and hopped over fallen logs. He was halfway to the little boy when I got a strong feeling in my gut that something terrible was going to happen.

"Michael! Michael!" I screamed but my voice was a whisper now, like I was yelling into a great big empty space. I looked at Angie. All the blood had drained from her face.

I squinted into the distance. The boy's mouth was moving faster, his eyes wide. *"Bad here! Bad!"*

Michael tripped once and got up, brushed himself off, and kept running. Finally he was right in front of the kid. Michael seemed to be shimmering too.

"Evil!" The child yelled. *"Evil!"*

Michael reached out a hand.

The boy vanished.

Michael patted around, looking this way and that, then turned to us. "Do you see him? Do you see him?" he yelled.

"No," Angie answered. It took us a few seconds to get down to where Michael was standing. It was chillier there and the air seemed very still. It smelled a little like smoke, as if some of the trees had been struck by bolts of lightning a long time ago and were still smoldering.

There was no one to be seen at all.

"Where … where could he go?" I asked. "There weren't any holes for him to fall into." We searched around. I thought I heard a whisper for a second or the sound of crying, but when I held myself perfectly still and listened, I heard nothing.

We split up and looked around. I made sure that the other two were always in my sight. After about ten minutes we met back where we had originally seen the boy.

"We better get home," I suggested.

"We can't just leave him," Angie said.

Michael examined the palm of his hand. "I don't think he was really here."

We both stared at him.

"I'll explain later. Let's start walking first."

We agreed and began heading back down the path.

It seemed to take years to get to Grandpa's cabin.

It wasn't until after we had eaten Grandpa's chicken soup and sandwiches and done dishes that Michael finally told us about the boy. We were in the living room. Angie had a blanket around her shoulders, though it wasn't really that cold. Grandpa was on the deck.

"When I touched him … " Michael started to explain. "… well, I really didn't touch him."

"What do you mean?" I asked. Michael's blue eyes, so like my own, looked troubled.

"My hand went right into him." He held out his hand, re-enacting the event. "He was — he was made of mist. And it was really, really cold. It was as if he was a ghost or something."

"There's no such thing as ghosts," Angie said.

"I know that," Michael huffed. "But there was something really strange about this boy."

"He probably just lives nearby," Angie suggested. "In a farmhouse or something."

"But he disappeared. Right in front of me. He couldn't have gone anywhere or run away. He just wasn't there anymore."

Angie shivered under her blanket. "A trick of the light.

It was kinda dark in there."

"I don't know," I said finally. "Maybe we should tell Grandpa."

They both looked at me. A moment of silence passed.

"At supper time," Michael answered. "I … I want to think about it more. He might believe all his stories went to our heads."

"Yeah, I want to go into town," Angie said, throwing off her blanket and getting up. "Walk around and see the sights — if there are any. Get away from all these trees and things. Maybe there's something fun going on. C'mon."

We followed her out the front door. I was quite happy to not think about the boy any longer. I needed time to clear my head.

Grandpa was sitting in his rocking chair, whittling. "Yeah, yeah, I know you're going to town. I heard Miss Loud-speaker announce it. I bet even my neighbors heard it." He flicked his knife and a long sliver of wood came off. I wondered what else he had heard. If he did know more, he didn't show it. "You three blurs don't slow down for a second, do you? It makes me tired just looking at you." He sent another chip skyward. I couldn't tell what he was carving. "Since you're going that way, would you mind picking me up a copy of this week's paper? Your ol' Grandpa Thursten would love that."

We agreed to do that and just as we were heading out of the yard, Grandpa yelled, "Don't fall in any holes — "

" — you might meet a rabbit you don't like." We finished it for him.

"Oh, you heard that one before."

We all laughed, then followed the road into Gimli.

"Grandpa sure hears a lot," Angie said when we were a safe distance from the house. "Doesn't he know old people are supposed to be deaf?"

"He can probably hear you right now," I said.

"No. He couldn't … could he?" Angie looked back. The cabin was quite far behind us.

"Well, the way you shout everything he could." Michael was grinning.

"I don't shout. I speak calmly and clearly."

"And loudly," I added.

Angie fumed. I knew she was searching for a perfect comeback, but her moment had passed. "You're both just jealous," she mumbled. We all chuckled for a second and continued onwards.

It took around forty-five minutes to walk into Gimli, past houses, cabins, trees, and more trees. Finally, we came over a small rise and there was the town itself laid out before us. It was really quite small compared to most towns in the U.S. And from this distance it appeared there wasn't very much going on.

But Michael and I had learned the previous year that looks could be deceiving. We'd found more than enough things to keep us entertained through our whole vacation.

The sun was warm and we strolled up and down the streets, looking in store windows and getting a feel for the place. A few people stared at us like we were escapees from an asylum. One old woman even looked up, saw us, then hobbled across to the other side of the street.

"Sarah," Michael said, "take a look at my forehead."

"Why?" I asked.

"Because I think there's a sign that says *Danger: American kids approaching.*"

We giggled and guffawed so hard we had to stop walking. This made a few more people stare at us. We noticed and started laughing some more. Then we headed down the street, holding our sides.

Already the events of the morning seemed far behind us, maybe even a daydream. We scouted around for an arcade or a park, but didn't have any luck, and I discovered I couldn't remember where anything was … almost as if the whole town had changed since last summer.

"What kind of place is this?" Angie asked. "It's as dull as math class. Is it against the law to have fun in Canada? And what kind of name is Gimli anyway?"

"Well …" I said, giving a long dramatic pause, "… I happen to know the answer to that. Grandpa told me this town is named after a gigantic hall where the old Viking gods would stay after the world ended. Kind of like a hotel for the big shots."

"Well, how come everyone's staring at us?" she asked.

"Cause they're Icelandic … just like us," I answered. "They like to stare and they like to tell long stories. Grandpa warned us about that last summer."

"So whatdaya think people from Gimli call themselves?" Michael asked.

"What do you mean?" Angie responded.

"Well, are they Gimli-ers and Gimli-ettes, or just plain Gimli-ites?"

"Michael, you're just plain stupid," I said.

"Just curious, that's all. Just using the scientific part of my mind."

"What mind?" Angie teased.

Michael rolled his eyes. "Just trying to teach you two how to think."

"Hey, look," I said. "Books."

We had come to a plain-looking bookstore at the end of an unremarkable street. The sign on the front said: *Odin's Eye Books*.

"I have a feeling I'm going to like this place," Michael said. We followed him inside.

The store was small, hot, cramped, and smelled like books. I loved it right away. The old woman at the till, who was half hidden in shadows, smiled at us and I felt instantly welcome. We rummaged around for awhile, pulling out novels, reading the back covers, then putting them back. Angie went straight to the romance section. I discovered a fantasy work I had been looking for and made my way to the front counter. I also picked up a copy of *The Interlake Spectator* from the pile that sat on the counter.

"That's a good book," the woman said softly. I looked up at her and almost dropped my money on the floor.

She only had one eye.

Her good eye was a swirling color of gray and I knew she could see right into my thoughts, right into the very center of my spirit. Her left eye was covered by a patch. She was in her sixties, her hair gray and tied in a bun, and she wore brown clothes.

"Uh ..." I said.

She grinned. Wrinkles formed around her eyes, made deep from years of smiling. "Don't worry. I know I look a little ... unique. I lost my eye a long time ago."

"Uh ... sorry."

She shrugged, her shoulders were wide. It seemed like she was made out of earth. "I see a lot more with one eye than I ever did with two. I guarantee it. By the way ... what's your name?"

"Sarah."

"Sarah who?"

"Sarah Asmundson."

She nodded for a moment. It was as if I had answered an unspoken question. "You've got Grettir's blood in your veins."

"Oh … do I? Uh … good."

"Here's your change." She opened a wrinkled hand. Coins seemed to appear magically in her palm. Had she even opened the till?

I took the quarters with shaky hands. They were warm.

"If you ever have any questions about anything in town … just ask me," she said. "I'm Althea, Gimli's answer lady."

"Sh–sure … see ya." Then I turned and went out the door, my brother and Angie following.

"Whoa — she was big time weird!" Angie exclaimed when we were a few blocks away. "The way her one eye just kinda glowed. Bizarre woman, that's for sure."

"You don't even know her!" I felt a little angry, but didn't know why.

"I could tell just by looking."

I fumed.

"Wake me when you kids are done fighting." Michael took *The Interlake Spectator* from me. "Let's see what's happening in this burg."

He made a show of opening the paper. We all looked at it.

The headline read: MYSTERIOUS DISAPPEARANCE RE-CALLED.

The picture beside the headline was of the boy we had seen that morning.

» 5 «

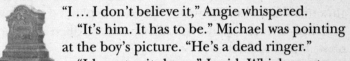"I … I don't believe it," Angie whispered.

"It's him. It has to be." Michael was pointing at the boy's picture. "He's a dead ringer."

"I have to sit down," I said. Which was true. My legs felt like they were suddenly transformed into wet clay. We went ahead to a small park and collapsed on a bench. Three pine trees cast three shadows across us and I shivered.

We read the article silently.

In the spring of 1941 young Eric Bardarson disappeared. The Bardarson family had been picnicking north of town. When they went to leave, their son had vanished. A search party was organized and though they spent the next few days searching, no trace of the boy was ever found. Donations to the Eric Bardarson Arts Scholarship are gratefully accepted.

"I told you he was a ghost," Michael said. "He has to be."

"It could still be some kind of trick." Angie didn't sound very sure of herself. "Couldn't it?"

"I don't know." I examined the picture of Eric. He was wearing what looked like a school uniform: a tie, a shirt and suit jacket, shorts, long socks, and black shoes. He looked exactly like the boy we had seen. The only difference was that he was smiling in the picture.

Staring at the photo made me feel uncomfortable. In it he was a happy, young kid who was probably thinking about playing baseball or riding his bike; he had no idea that in a few days he would disappear forever.

Well, not exactly forever. If he was some sort of spirit.

I glanced at the rest of the front page. There was something about city taxes and a festival named *Islendingadagurinn* and at the bottom of the page was a grainy picture of a dead cow. The article below it explained that this cow, like several others recently, had been killed and had all its blood sucked out.

What kind of town was this?

I got off the bench, stepped out into the sunlight. I didn't want to be cold anymore. "This is all way, way too weird."

Both Angie and Michael stood too. Michael folded up the paper. "Yeah, I'll say. Last year all we did was suntan, roller blade, and go fishing. And listen to Grandpa's stories."

I crossed my arms. "We had better tell Grandpa tonight, for sure. Even if he thinks we're just being stupid, crazy kids."

Michael and Angie nodded in agreement. They followed me down the sidewalk and we started trying to find our way out of town.

"Hey! Hello there!" someone yelled from behind us.

We turned around. Standing by the bench we were just on, waving a plastic bag, was a blonde-haired guy who looked about fifteen. He was wearing a black T-shirt and blue-jean shorts. He was as tall as Michael but very stocky.

"Hey!" he repeated.

It took me a moment to realize the bag he was holding was mine. With the book I had just bought. He started coming towards us.

"You forgot this," he said when we were face to face. He had blue eyes and was grinning. His face was tanned.

"Oh … thanks," I answered as I took the bag. "I'd have been mad at myself if I lost it — hey, how'd you know it was my book?"

"You look like the bookish type." His grin got even bigger, revealing straight white teeth.

I wasn't sure if that was a compliment or not.

"I mean it in the nicest way possible." Was he reading my mind? I noticed that his hair was shaved at the sides like a skate boarder's. He looked familiar, almost like someone I had seen on TV. "You three are new in town, aren't you?"

"How could you tell?" Michael asked. "Is it stamped on our foreheads?"

"No. I know most everyone around here who's my age. This place fills up with tourists and visitors in the summer. Besides, your shirt has the Dallas Cowboys on it … we're all Blue Bomber fans here."

"Who?" Michael's face became a living question mark.

"Winnipeg's football team."

"I've heard of them," I said, even though I hadn't. I just wanted him to look at me. "We're from Missouri."

"Missouri? How come you don't have accents? Why don't you say *Y'all* and all that stuff."

"Why don't you say *eh* all the time?" Michael asked.

"Uh …" he paused, still grinning. "I see what you mean."

"We grew up in Montana," I explained.

"*They* grew up in Montana," Angie added. "I'm from North Dakota."

He looked at her and I felt a twinge of jealousy. "My name's Brand." This time when he smiled, dimples formed in his cheeks.

We all introduced ourselves and Brand shook everyone's hand. He had a firm, warm shake and I didn't want to let go. Angie winked at me when Brand wasn't looking and I almost blushed.

"So where you guys staying?" Brand asked.

"With our Grandpa, Thursten," Michael answered.

Brand laughed. "Ol' Thursten. Does he still tell that story about the headless barmaid?"

"Yes," I answered. "Do you know Grandpa?"

"He used to recite stories to us kids at school. We'd all have nightmares later. He's really good friends with my grandmother. They sit and talk Icelandic to each other. Can't understand a word they say ... except when they point at me and say *akarn* every once in awhile."

"Akarn?" Michael asked.

"Little acorn. That's what they call me. He's a fun old guy."

There was silence for a moment. Brand kept grinning through it all. He ran his hand through his hair. It went back to its original position. "Well I have to go. If you guys come into town and want me to show you around, you can find me at *Ye Ol' Ice Cream Shoppe*. I work there most days."

"We will," I said, maybe a little too enthusiastically.

Then he turned and was gone, striding down the street.

Angie looked at me and raised her eyebrows. "Well, well, well ... I think I sense a crush coming up."

"Oh, c'mon," I answered. "We just met him."

"And?"

"And ... and we better get back to Grandpa's."

Angie laughed. I knew it wouldn't be the last time she would tease me about Brand. We started walking out of town.

When we got back to the cabin, Grandpa wasn't on the deck. There were lots of wood chips so he'd obviously been busy. We went through the front door.

"Grandpa, we're home!" Michael announced.

No answer.

"Maybe you should yell, Angie," he suggested. "He always hears you."

Angie frowned. "Ha. Ha. Ha."

We poked our heads into each room, called out his name. Still nothing. It was almost funny, each of us following the others around like three miniature stooges, opening doors, yelling, closing doors. Except I was beginning to get a little worried. Grandpa hadn't said anything about going anywhere.

"Oh great, we've lost him," Angie exclaimed, collapsing into a sofa chair. "How are we going to explain this to our parents? We lost Grandpa ... but we had a great holiday."

"I told you a bizillion times, don't exaggerate!" Michael stretched out on the couch and yawned, his mouth became a gaping O. "He's got to be around here somewhere. He likely stepped out with one of his friends. They're telling each other big long stories about giant snakes or dead people right now. That's all they seem to talk about around here."

I sat in the other chair. "You're probably right." I covered my mouth as I yawned. It had been a long day already. I settled myself down, relaxing my body. I glanced at Michael and Angie; both had their eyes closed. We all deserved a nap, I figured. I let my eyelids slowly slide together.

I drifted into a vast warm darkness. A moment later a dream worked its way into that black space. I was suddenly stumbling through a thick forest of trees at twilight. Ghostly wisps of fog drifted ahead of me, catching the light of the moon. I wandered for a time, shivering and looking ahead. I wanted to go back, to get out of the trees, but something was pulling me forward, one step at a time.

I saw a figure in the distance and so I headed towards it. With each movement I was growing lighter, until my feet were no longer touching the ground. A wind had come up, pulling me a few feet above the earth and making me float.

I came closer, moving faster now. The figure was the boy: Eric.

Go away! he was waving his hand at me. *Bad here! Go away!*

He motioned harder, now he was yelling but I couldn't hear him. He looked very frightened. As I passed him I could see tears in his eyes.

Big, ghostly tears.

And I knew he was crying for me. Crying because he must know what lay ahead, where I was going. How bad can it be when a ghost is weeping for you?

I floated past and I couldn't even turn my head to look behind me.

A few seconds later I saw it.

A cabin. A very old cabin. Maybe one of the first ones built in this area. All logs and a sod roof, but the floor had sunk in on one side so it leaned crazily, the door at an odd angle. I knew there was darkness inside those four walls, that every nightmare I'd ever had was nothing compared to what waited through that doorway. I kept coming, heading straight at the door, gaining speed.

It opened.

And I was swept inside, into pitch blackness. Cold, smelly air surrounded me. The door slammed shut and I fell to a soggy floor. I pushed myself up and something wet squished below my hands. I sucked in my breath, felt my lungs tighten.

I couldn't breathe. I was suffocating.

Then something started to slam on the door.

And I knew the dark evil thing was outside, wanting to get back in. Into its own home.

It banged against the door. Harder.

And harder.

The wood splintered into pieces. Then there was a dark blur of motion, two eyes glowing, two arms reaching for me.

Then I found air, snapped awake.

I was up out of the chair and standing on the floor. Alive. Heart beating. Breathing. In and out, like they were my first breaths ever. Once. Twice. Three times.

My heart wouldn't slow down.

Both Michael and Angie were still asleep. I looked around. I was okay, everything was going to be alright.

This was the real world.

The door to Grandpa's house swung open and banged against the wall.

A wolf was standing there, its gray soulless eyes staring right into mine.

» 7 «

I screamed. Michael shot straight up into the air. So did Angie.

"What! What! What is it?" Michael asked, squinting at me, sleepy and angry at the same time. Then he saw the animal, its mouth open showing huge glistening teeth. Michael jumped off the couch and backed away. "Nice puppy … *nice puppy.*" It looked from me to Michael to Angie, trying to decide which one it was going to swallow whole first.

I held myself completely still.

"Who in the blazes is doing all the screaming?" asked the wolf.

I shook my head. Was I still dreaming?

Grandpa stepped into the doorway, standing behind the creature. He was carrying a shotgun. "Somebody answer me! Who is yelling to wake the dead? Was it you, Angie?" He reached down and patted the wolf's head. It arched its neck to give him a better angle.

Grandpa walked inside the house. "Well?"

"Uh …" I started. "It was me. I … uh … was dreaming and the … the wolf was just there and so …"

"Wolf?" He scratched his head. "Oh, Hugin here. He's

only part wolf. He's half German Shepherd too. Scared you, did he?"

"Y-yes."

"Well … it's good to be scared. Let's you know you're alive. Bet your heart's beating like crazy now."

It was. I was going to wear it out before I turned sixteen.

Grandpa went to the closet and put his shotgun away. He locked the door, put the key in his pocket, and turned back to us.

"What were you doing?" I asked.

"Just poking around in the bushes. Thought I heard something out there this afternoon. So I borrowed Hugin here from a friend of mine and we went out tracking."

"Did you find anything?" Michael asked. His voice sounded squeaky. Like he couldn't catch his breath.

"I think you need a drink of water, son." Grandpa cocked one eyebrow. "Or has your voice always been so high pitched?"

"No — " Michael squeaked, then paused to cough. "No," he said in a deeper tone.

Grandpa nodded. "That's better. Now what was the question … oh yeah. I didn't find anything. Just a few broken branches and what looked like tracks."

"Tracks for what?" Angie was still watching the dog.

"I couldn't tell. I tried to follow them, and I thought Hugin had the scent, but, after bumping through the bush for a few hundred yards, he just turned and looked at me, barked a couple times like he was reciting the dog alphabet, then he ran straight home. So I followed."

Michael sat down. "Did something spook him?"

"No. There's nothing in that big ol' world out there that will spook Hugin. I think he came back to the house cause he thought it would be safer for me. Guess we'll never know what was out there. A bear, most likely."

Hugin padded across the floor and sniffed at my feet. "Does he bite?" I asked.

"He hasn't bit anyone this week as far as I know. Though he ate a kid whole last week. The kid was trespassing, though." Grandpa went into the kitchen. Why couldn't he just answer questions with yes or no? He was worse than us teenagers.

I reached down and patted Hugin's head. It seemed about ten times as big as my hand, hard and padded with thick fur. I got down and looked eye to eye with him and he licked my face. It didn't take me long to realize that I liked this dog. My father made his living training bird dogs, so I knew a good dog when I saw one.

Even one that was part wolf.

I could tell Hugin was more than just a normal canine. He was a king: noble, strong, and proud. The type of dog who'd drag you out of an avalanche or a burning building.

I sat back on the couch and Hugin nuzzled against my legs, pinning me there, forcing me to pat him. Angie joined me and Hugin began wagging his thick gray-and-black tail, quite happy to have so much attention.

I could hear Grandpa banging around the kitchen, glass clinking. He came out a few minutes later, a pot of tea in one hand and cups in the other.

"Who's Grettir?" I asked as he set the tea on the coffee table.

"Grettir? Why?"

"That old lady at the bookstore said I had Grettir's blood in my veins."

"Oh … Althea." He shook a finger at me. "I warned you about the folks in Gimli. They'll talk your ear off if you give them half a chance. Then they'll move to the other one. And she's the worst of them all." He lifted up the tea pot, motioned with it. "Hugin here belongs to her. She named him after one of Odin's ravens. It means thought — he's supposed to be faster than the speed of thought. Which isn't very fast in your case, Michael."

"Geez! Thanks, Grandpa!" Michael crossed his arms.

"Nice comeback, kiddo." Grandpa began pouring tea into a cup. "Anyone else?" he asked when he was finished. I can't say I much like tea, but a warm drink was exactly what I needed.

"Sure," I said.

"Well, pour it yourself." He laughed and sat back. "Grettir, Grettir, Grettir." He took a sip from his tea cup. "She's picked an old name ... he might even be an ancestor of ours. Grettir Asmundson he was called or Grettir the strong."

"When did he live?" I was pouring my own tea. Hugin had abandoned Angie and me for Michael's attention.

"I don't know exactly. The stories written about him date back to the 1300s, but he lived long before then. He was supposed to be one of the strongest men in Iceland. As far as I can remember, he just fought most of his life, recklessly. Though he was supposed to be a nice guy too — well, nice in a Viking kind of way. He even battled mound dwellers and supernatural monsters because human foes weren't tough enough for him. But that proved his undoing because one day he locked horns with a monster who was too much for him."

"You mean he lost?" Angie asked.

"No, not exactly. You see, he decided to try and wrestle a particularly mean thrall."

"Thrall?" I asked.

"An undead man. This happened a lot in Iceland in the

old days. People just didn't seem to want to stay dead. They hung around and made a lot of noise and broke things. This thrall was a cruel bitter sheep herder who had died mysteriously the night before Christmas — I think his name was Glam. He came back from the dead and started haunting the farmer he had been working for.

"Anyway, Grettir had heard about him and decided to spend a night at the farmhouse. He hid in a big fur blanket and waited. After about a third of the night had passed, something huge banged on the roof, then kicked in the door. It stomped across the floor and grabbed the fur. Grettir held on and the blanket ripped in two between them. Then they wrestled with each other so hard that they broke the door frame and the roof of the house and rolled outside, under the moon. Grettir was stronger and he overpowered the thrall and knelt on his chest. With his last bit of strength, Glam put a curse on Grettir so that from that point on, anything Grettir did with his strength would only lead to bad luck. Then Grettir lopped off his head … kind of messy but it's the only way to kill these thralls, I guess. Grettir later was outlawed as a murderer and had to spend his last days on Drang Isle, a cold desolate place. I think there was a price on his head and someone finally murdered him, even cut off his hand after he was dead. Just to get him to release his sword."

"That doesn't sound like a very happy ending," Angie said.

"It was his life. The old sagas aren't Hollywood movies. They're gritty. Full of blood and smoke and tough characters. Kind of like the people who settled Iceland. And Gimli, come to think of it."

"So we're supposed to be related to this Grettir?" I asked.

"There's a good chance we are. I'll have to go back to

the homeland sometime and look up our family trees. Maybe at the next big Asmundson reunion."

"We are related to him," I said suddenly.

Grandpa looked at me. "Why do you say that?"

"Uh …" I hesitated, trying to understand what I had meant. "It's just a gut feeling. When you told the story, I felt like I was there … with him."

Everyone stared at me. Grandpa smiled. "You may be right," he said. "Do you ever get any other gut feelings that come true?"

"Um … no," I said. I wasn't quite sure what he meant. "I don't think so."

He stared at me for a long moment then nodded to himself. What had he figured out? He set down his cup. "Did any of you three happen to pick up a paper for me?"

"Uh …" Michael started.

Grandpa looked at him. "Uh … did you, or didn't you?"

"We did," Michael continued. He got the paper and handed it to Grandpa. "But before you read it there's something we have to tell you."

"Actually," Michael said a second later, "maybe you should take a look at the paper first."

Grandpa shook his head. Clearly he didn't have a clue what we were talking about. "Open the paper, close the paper — what's going on here? All three of you look like you just missed being run over by a big Mac truck."

"Please," I asked.

He must have heard the frightened tone of my voice. He opened *The Interlake Spectator* and looked at it for some time. Then he glanced at us. "Is it the dead cow story? Don't tell me you guys really did it. Here I thought it was just aliens." He laughed.

"No ... see the boy there." Michael pointed.

"Yes."

"We saw him this morning."

Grandpa's face hardened. "You what?"

"Well ..." Michael began, then he explained how we had wandered into the trees and everything that had happened to us after that. Grandpa looked serious but didn't speak a word until Michael was finished. He set the paper down, rose slowly from the chair as if some of his strength had been sapped. He went to the back door, pulled the curtain aside, and stared out. He stayed that way for a full minute.

Michael, Angie, and I looked quizzically at each other. "What — " I started to ask.

Grandpa turned towards us. His eyes were cold and very serious. "You're going home tomorrow," he announced.

"What?" we exclaimed in unison.

He came a few steps closer. "I said, you're going home tomorrow. I'll call your parents tonight. Till then, no one leaves this house. Do you understand?"

"No, I don't understand," I said. "Why are you sending us home? What did we do?"

"You didn't do anything. It's just that … business has come up. I can't look after you anymore."

"What business?" Michael asked. His frown mirrored my own.

"I have to go away for a few days. Look after some things. Old unfinished things. So you three will be heading home."

"But — " I started.

"No buts. This is the way it has to be. I'm sorry, but I forgot about this … business." His face softened. He spoke gently. " You can stay even longer next summer. Okay? All summer if you want. We'll have twice as much fun."

It sounded like he was trying to bribe us.

"Okay?" He repeated.

We were all in shock. "Uh … sure," Michael answered. What could we do?

"It's settled, then." Grandpa smiled. "I really am sorry, believe me." He leaned over, picked up the tea pot and the empty cups, and started back towards the kitchen. Hugin padded after him, then Grandpa whispered a few words in another language. The dog obediently turned around and sat in the middle of the room.

Almost as if he was told to keep an eye on us.

Angie looked quite upset. I was about to say something to her when Grandpa came back into the room. "I have to go out for a few minutes." He was putting his hat on — a Toronto Blue Jays cap. "Will you three do me a favor? Will you just stay in the house? I … I think it might have been a bear I heard this afternoon."

We nodded. Grandpa said something else to Hugin. The dog looked at him, then back at us. Then the door closed softly behind Grandpa.

Michael crossed his arms. "Well that was very, ultra bizarre."

"That's for sure." Angie had her arms crossed too and seemed to be shivering. "I've never seen him like this before. What did we do to get sent home?"

I just couldn't stand to sit anymore. I got up and paced the floor. "I don't think we did anything. I think … well … I don't know. That he's trying to protect us," I said.

Michael motioned and Hugin padded over to him. The dog rubbed up against his knees. "I have a feeling you're right. There's something wrong. The fact that we saw that gho — that kid really bothered him."

"And what was he out looking for today?" Angie had her feet up on the couch now and was hugging her knees. "Was it really a bear?"

"And why is this dog so smart?" I asked. I noticed that Hugin was turning his head as each of us spoke, as if he understood every word. He looked at me and it seemed like he was smiling.

"Well, I don't want to go home," Michael announced. "We just got here. I am not going to take another long, stupid bus ride. It's not fair."

"I don't know if we have a choice," I said. I leaned against the wall next to the mantel. At eye level was a picture of

Grandma and Grandpa, both in fishing gear. Maybe if she were still alive she'd explain what was going on. She was always so good to us kids.

"Maybe we can talk to him," Angie suggested.

I shook my head. "I don't think so. You saw the look on his face. It was almost as if he was frightened."

Hugin's ears perked up. He rose and walked past me, brushing my legs.

"Grandpa doesn't get frightened — nothing scares Grandpa," Angie said.

"I know … but … he just seemed that way. For a second. Maybe just frightened for us is what I mean."

"You know — " Michael started.

He stopped. Hugin was barking, loud and strong, at the back door.

» 9 «

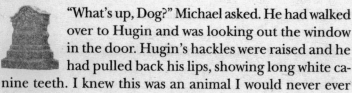"What's up, Dog?" Michael asked. He had walked over to Hugin and was looking out the window in the door. Hugin's hackles were raised and he had pulled back his lips, showing long white canine teeth. I knew this was an animal I would never ever want mad at me. "What is it, boy? What do you hear?" Michael reached for the door.

"Don't open that!" I yelled.

Michael frowned. "Why?"

"Grandpa said we're supposed to stay inside. And because … because you don't know what's out there."

Michael rolled his eyes. "I looked out the window. There's nothing in the backyard, Sis. The dog probably hears a raccoon or something. They have raccoons here, don't they?" Michael turned the knob and slowly pulled the door open.

"Don't!" This time it was Angie.

Michael ignored us both and stepped into the doorway. Hugin stood beside him, barking even harder, so his whole body seemed to shake. Then he switched to a low angry growl. "I … I don't believe it … it's … gigantic," Michael exclaimed. His eyes were wide and frightened. He stepped out the door. Hugin followed. "It's … oh no. OH NO! IT'S

GOT A HOLD OF ME!"

"Michael!" I ran to the door. "Michael!"

He was gone. Hugin was about halfway across the yard, snarling at the trees. "Michael!" I yelled. Angie had joined me. "Where — "

"Surprise!" Michael popped up from a bush beside us. We screamed in unison and Michael rolled on the ground laughing. "Got you! Got you!"

"That's not funny!" I yelled when I had caught my breath.

"It was to me." Michael was standing now, holding his side. "We all needed a good laugh."

"Neither of us laughed." Angie had one hand on her hip.

"Well, I sure did." Michael was brushing the grass off his pants. "I got a big hardy-har-har out of it."

"Look at Hugin." I pointed. He was at the edge of Grandpa's yard, where the grass gave way to huge pine trees. He was barking and growling crazily. I noticed the fence gate was open. "Something really is out there."

Michael looked. "Bah. It's probably nothing. Though he's sure barking a lot."

"C'mere, Hugin," I called. The dog looked my way, then continued growling. "Come on, boy." He ignored me.

I took a deep breath and started walking towards him.

"Sarah, what are you doing?" Angie asked.

"Just getting the dog," I answered, but my voice was so hoarse that I don't know if she heard me. Each step was impossible to take, but I pushed myself ahead. Some part of me refused to be scared.

I stared at the open gate. Beyond the tall fence was thick underbrush and more trees, all darkened by afternoon shadows. Anything could be in there, I realized.

Sarah, don't be stupid, I told myself. Turn around and go back to the house.

But I couldn't. Not without Hugin.

A few steps later I was beside him. He was growling even louder as if trying to ward something away.

I trudged past him. Closer to the gate, closer. I couldn't seem to stop myself.

"Sarah!" This time it was Michael. But he sounded so far away, like he was yelling from the end of a long tunnel. I could barely hear him.

Hugin stayed behind me. Barking now, maybe trying to warn me. Was he frozen to the spot?

I felt a chill. The temperature was plunging to the freezing mark here at this end of the yard. Even my bones were getting cold.

Still I carried on. The gate loomed in front of me. I had this awful fear that I was going to walk right through it, out into the wilderness, and never return again. There was a whispering sound just beyond the fence. Almost like breathing.

Or was someone calling my name? An ancient, raspy voice.

Hugin stopped barking. Or maybe I couldn't hear him anymore.

I reached the gate. It took all my will to stop my feet from moving. I extended my arm, my fingers dull and cold.

With all the strength I could muster, I pulled on the gate. It closed slowly, squeaking and whining. For a moment I thought I saw a dark rustling shape moving outside, then with a *click* the gate was shut.

I stepped back. There was dirt on the top part of the gate. It almost looked like a hand print.

I took another step back. Hugin renewed his barking, ran up to me, and leaned against me, growling. Something in the solidness of his body gave me strength. I turned around.

Both Angie and Michael were standing there, staring at me.

I walked towards them.

"What were you doing?" Michael asked when I got closer.

"I — I just had to close it," I said. "If I didn't ... well I don't know ..."

I kept going towards the cabin. "Let's go inside," I said. "I've had enough excitement for one day."

I called once from the doorway and Hugin came running. I felt relieved when all of us were inside. Michael and Angie sat down, but I couldn't take my eyes away from the window. Hugin stayed by the closed door, no longer growling. He just seemed to be waiting.

A few minutes later Grandpa came through the front door, hugging a bulging bag of groceries. Celery stalks peeked out the top. "You three weren't going anywhere were you?" he asked when he saw me by the back door.

"Uh ... no," I answered.

Hugin barked once and Grandpa walked over to him. He said a few soothing words in Icelandic, then patted the dog on its head. Hugin wagged his tail and settled down by the back door.

Grandpa winked at us. "Well ... I got the fixings for a wonderful meal. I'd appreciate some help in the kitchen."

And so we helped cook supper, slicing carrots, celery, and onions for a beef stew. I found I was glad to be doing something to take my mind away from the fact that we would be leaving tomorrow. The kitchen filled with the smells of cooking food; aromas that reminded me of being at home with my parents on those cool winter nights in Missouri.

None of us spoke while we made supper. Even Grandpa was quiet, he only opened his mouth to say, "Cut enough carrots for a hundred rabbits. You guys will have the best eyesight in all America." I set the table, trying not to let the cutlery clink. It was almost as if there was someone in the other room whom we didn't want to wake up.

Once Hugin made a whining sound then stopped. I glanced and saw that he was resting his head on the floor. But his eyes were still sharply fixed on the door.

We sat down to eat a few minutes later. The stew was wonderful, with thick gravy, tender meat, a layer of dumplings, and more vegetables than I could care to count. It was like the first time I had ever tasted stew — as if everything was brand new.

"This is very, very good," Angie said. I guess I wasn't the only one enjoying the meal.

"Yeah, it is," Michael agreed. "But there's enough garlic in here to knock out a vampire."

Grandpa narrowed his eyes, looking serious. "Just eat it all up," he commanded gruffly. "Okay?"

"Uh ... sure." Michael was scooping up another forkful. "I — actually like garlic, Grandpa."

"Good boy. Good for you." Grandpa was smiling again. "It's good for your health ... but bad for your breath."

We chuckled half-heartedly. Angie shot me a quick look that seemed to say: *has Grandpa gone bonkers?*

When we were finished eating, Grandpa cleared his throat. "Tonight you're all going to sleep in the main guest room."

"What?" I set down my glass. "We can't sleep in the same room as Michael."

Grandpa smiled. "You're going to have to put up with his snoring for one night."

"I don't snore!"

"Why do we have to sleep together?" Angie asked.

"I need the other spare room. There's work I have to do."

"Why do we have to go home?" I asked.

"Because there's business I forgot. I can't look after you and do it too."

"What business?"

"My business," he said with finality. "Will you three do dishes? I have to make a few phone calls."

Grandpa got up and went to the phone hanging on the living room wall. We went into the kitchen. Michael washed while Angie and I dried. From where I was standing I could hear Grandpa on the phone. I moved a little closer.

I caught the tail end of the conversation. "No. I can't explain. You'll have to take my word for it, Robert." Then he hung up. He had obviously been talking to Mom and Dad. I wished I had been listening a little earlier.

He picked up the phone and dialed again. I edged closer to the wall.

"It's taking you a long time to dry that dish," Michael said.

I motioned him to be quiet.

He turned back to the sink, muttering, "If you want to be lazy, go ahead."

I strained my ears. Grandpa was talking in another language on the phone. Icelandic, I assumed, because every second word had a *th* or a *grr* sound. I could tell by the tone of his voice that he was upset. He had taught me a few Icelandic words, mostly put-downs, but I couldn't pick anything out of what he was saying. He paused for a second and I assumed he was listening to whoever was on the other end of the line.

"*Neinn,*" he said suddenly. "*Draugr.*"

I caught my breath.

"*Draugr,*" he repeated. Hugin pricked up his ears.

I knew that word. Why was Grandpa saying it?

He started whispering now and no matter how hard I

tried, I couldn't hear what he was saying. A moment later he hung up the phone and I quickly went to the sink, picked up a dish, and started drying.

"Aren't you done yet?" Grandpa asked. He was in the doorway, smiling.

"We would be but Sarah's too slow," Michael said.

I kicked him.

"She's just careful that's all." Grandpa was still smiling. It seemed a little unreal — he was forcing himself to look happy. I thought I could see something in his eyes though, a kind of haggard look. Like he was very tired but just putting on a nice face for the company. "It's all set up. Your mom and dad will pick you up from the bus back at home."

"Oh … good," I said.

"Yes, it is. I really am sorry things worked out this way, kids. I was looking forward to having you three around." He turned. "Now if you'll excuse me, I've got a few things to do."

He left. When we finished the dishes we went out to the front room. Grandpa must have been in the back room. It sounded like he was banging on something metal. Occasionally I caught the smell of burning wood.

"What's he doing?" Angie asked.

"Who knows." Michael sat back. "I think he's gone a little loco."

"It's hard to believe our holiday will be over tomorrow." Angie was looking down. "Over even before it started."

We were all quiet. Grandpa was silent too. Whatever he'd been doing was done. He came walking out carrying Michael's suitcase. "I got your stuff here, Michael." He set it down. "Well," he announced. "It's bed time."

"Bed time? It's only eight o'clock!" Michael exclaimed.

"Eight fifteen, actually. And you've got to get on the bus early. You don't want to argue with 'ol Gramps on your last night here, do you?"

I did. But I kept my mouth closed.

"We're all going to need a good sleep tonight," Grandpa added.

I changed into my nightgown in the bathroom. About fifteen minutes later we were all settled in our beds; Angie and I in one, Michael in the other next to the small window.

Grandpa knocked on the door then poked his head in. "Lock this tonight, will you? And if you hear anything … whatever it is … don't leave this room." He paused. "Goodnight."

He closed the door.

10

"What on earth was that all about?" Angie asked. She was hugging her pillow. "I'm starting to get freaked out."

"You're not the only one — but I am going to lock the door." I rolled out of bed and twisted the key on the door, then turned the handle and pulled to be sure it was locked. I tugged the old iron key out of the keyhole. It was about six inches long and heavy. I set it on the bedside table and crawled back under the blankets. "Maybe we should board up the window too."

"There's something really wrong here." Michael was sitting up in the other bed. "Grandpa's just not acting like himself." He flipped his hair back out of his eyes. "I wonder if … like … he's getting senile or something? Or Alzheimer's?"

"Alzheimer's is when you forget things," Angie said.

"You know what I mean. Maybe he's sick."

"I don't think so." I paused, trying to find the right words. "I think it's something worse. Well, this may be nothing, but after he phoned Mom and Dad he called someone else and talked in Icelandic. The only word I understood was *draugr.*"

"You mean … like … from his story?" Angie was squeezing the pillow even closer.

"Yeah, that same word. It might not mean anything. And I might have heard it wrong … but I don't think so."

Michael looked right at me. "Sarah, you don't really believe that story was true, do you?"

"No … but Grandpa thinks something's going on like that story or that involves it. I don't know. It's all a little confusing. He is scared of something, though."

"What can we do?" Angie asked.

I shrugged. "Wait until morning, I guess. What do you think, Michael?"

"You're right. That's all we can do." He settled himself below the covers. "I know one thing … it's going to be hard to go to sleep tonight. Mega hard."

"Should we … should we leave the light on?" I asked. They both looked at me, their faces pale.

"No," Michael said finally. "I'd feel like a little kid." He reached over and clicked it off.

The room went completely black. "Uh … goodnight everyone," I whispered.

"Goodnight," they echoed.

Hope I see you in the morning, I thought to myself.

It took a moment for my eyes to adjust to the darkness. A silver beam of moonlight came in through the thin curtains, projecting an image of the window on my wall. It was obviously a full moon tonight.

Which didn't make me feel good at all.

I couldn't relax. I kept glancing back and forth, back and forth, from one side of the room to the other. I'm not sure what I was looking for.

But at some point my eyes must have gotten tired, because I fell asleep. And this time I didn't dream. There was only darkness within deeper darkness.

I awoke suddenly. It took me a moment to remember where

I was and that in a few short hours I'd be on a bus heading home. How much time had passed? Was it midnight yet?

I saw that the moonlight had moved farther down the wall. It seemed brighter and the shadow of the window was larger. Was the moon coming closer to the earth?

I could hear Angie's soft rhythmic breathing beside me. Michael was snoring.

I laughed quietly to myself. A low, nasally, grumbling sound came from his side of the room like low thunder. Poor Michael, he always thought he was so perfect. Now I finally had something to tease him about. All the way home I could imitate his buzzsaw snoring. That would help the trip go faster.

His wheezy inhalations got worse, became thicker and deeper like he had suddenly developed a really bad cold. He wasn't going to choke was he? Didn't some people die from snoring too loud? Or too long?

Or was it they forgot to breathe?

Gradually I realized the snoring sounded more like deep, throaty growling.

Not coming from Michael at all. But beyond him.

Outside the window.

A dark shadow was creeping slowly across the wall. A twisted, bulky shape edged up to the windowpane, blocking the moonlight. The silhouette grew larger. I tried to move my neck, to look towards the window, but all the strength had been drained from my body.

Boards moaned as if something huge had leaned its weight on the outside wall, trying to get closer.

To see what was inside.

Then I heard a sharp scraping noise like a nail being drawn against glass. Digging a deep groove.

I still couldn't budge. A cold Arctic mass of air crept into the room and was freezing me in place, slowing the blood in my veins, the thoughts in my head. I was trapped, helpless. I just stared at the shadow on the wall.

Angie wasn't breathing anymore. At least I couldn't hear her.

"Angie?" I whispered, my voice hoarse, my lips sluggish. It was hard to find the air to speak. "Michael?"

They didn't answer. I tried to move my arm, to jostle Angie awake. I could only edge it slowly towards her, an inch at a time. It was becoming very hard to concentrate. I felt, oddly enough, like sleeping — that all I really needed to do was close my eyes and rest and everything would go away.

I knew I couldn't surrender to this drowsiness. It was a sleep that would leave me in darkness forever.

My heartbeat slowed. My eyelids grew heavier. I didn't seem to have the energy to stop them from sliding shut.

The house creaked. Even more weight was leaning on it now. The low rumbling outside the window grew louder.

With a huge effort I moved my hand an inch to my left and touched Angie's arm.

She was ice cold.

"Angie," I whispered. *"Angie, wake up."*

No reaction. Not even a whisper. And I couldn't find enough strength to shake her. It was getting harder and harder to stay awake. I blinked and my heavy, tired eyes stayed closed for what must have been a minute.

When I opened them again I could hear a soft sliding sound.

The window was being opened! I was sure of it. Slowly, quietly opened.

Then came a wet, hollow breathing. My limbs, my chest, everything had stopped working. I couldn't even feel really frightened except inside my head. I had to keep myself awake. Somehow.

The window slid higher, letting in a chilling breeze.

And with it came colder and colder air. Not outside air, but something far different, from another age, another place. Air from cellars a hundred years old. From dark caves. From the deep undisturbed chambers inside burial mounds. Heavy with the scent of dirt. It spilled into our room.

Every time I inhaled, my lungs grew emptier so that I needed more air.

My breathing slowed.

My eyes closed again.

It took all my willpower to open them, to stop the sleep from settling in on me.

Now there was no moonlight. Only darkness. Whatever was outside the window had blocked it completely. It must be huge.

Then came a cracking sound of boards slowly being broken as the window frame was tested. The shadowy shape was too big to fit through that space. And yet it was forcing itself inside.

I knew the boards wouldn't hold for long.

I moved my arm closer to Angie, found her hand. It was frozen, each finger made of ice. I imagined mine felt the same. But one of those icicles seemed to move. Was she awake too? Lying as paralyzed as me?

Maybe together, somehow, we could get out of this. Even if we could scream, that would be something.

I tried to open my mouth, to whisper to her, but my lips wouldn't budge. I concentrated on squeezing her hand, but my fingers hardly moved at all.

A board snapped and part of the house surrendered to this outside force. Glass shattered, slowly. I could hear each creaking, cracking sound like ice breaking up in spring, then the tinkling sound of the glass hitting the floor piece by piece.

I had stopped breathing ages ago.

Another huge wooden crack was followed by a third one. Bits of plaster fell down. Then a fourth crack and a fifth. And I knew it was almost in the room, it was succeeding.

A smell floated into my nostrils, a stench of rotting meat and spoiled milk, of old urine and smoke. Inescapable and heavy.

The intruder was sniffing now, probably at the edge of Michael's bed. It paused only to growl. I knew it was searching, that it couldn't quite see us. The window was still creaking and cracking, so it wasn't all the way in the room yet.

A window smashed in some distant part of the cabin.

I thought I heard Michael moan in pain.

Then Hugin started barking, outside. The deep sound of his warning brought me further away from sleep. I tried to move, but failed.

There was a loud growl in our room, low, angry, and threatening. The boards smashed and cracked. Plaster fell in on me from the ceiling.

Doors slammed here and there inside the house — Grandpa! He yelled something I couldn't understand. A name. Or was he swearing?

He knocked over a table. Glass shattered. Then he slammed another door. He seemed to be desperately searching for something.

Hugin was closer now. His snarling sounded muffled. Did he have a hold of something?

Suddenly there was a final crack of wood, a retreating throaty roar, and the remains of the window slammed shut, echoing through the room.

The thing was gone. I couldn't turn my head, but I knew it had turned away from us to face the dog.

Hugin was struggling with something — someone —

just outside our room.

I found I could move my eyes slightly, but my head refused to budge. From the angle where I was lying I could see the edge of the window and not much more. Half the curtains were off, had been knocked to the ground. It looked like the window had been broken along with a lot of the wall around it.

The back door slammed. Grandpa wasn't going outside was he?

Grandpa! Don't! I wanted to yell. Instead I just mouthed the words. My lips were too cold to move.

But the room seemed to get warmer. Or my body was. I could move slowly. I squeezed Angie's hand.

She squeezed back, weakly.

Something huge slammed into the side of the house. Boards crashed, our wall shook and threatened to topple in.

My heart started beating again. I could breathe, too.

Grandpa started yelling again. In Icelandic. Short harsh words.

He *was* outside. What was he doing out there?

I discovered I could move my neck now and I turned. The window had been smashed in, the remaining torn dirty curtains were fluttering in the breeze. I couldn't see outside. Both Angie and Michael were lying with their eyes open, their faces pale.

"Guys …" my voice was a hoarse whisper, my throat dry, "can you hear me?"

Angie gave me a muffled, *"Yes."*

"I … I can't move," Michael whispered. "Sarah, why … can't I move?"

"I don't know," I answered. "But I think Grandpa needs our help."

"I dreamed something had a hold of my leg," Michael

said. I could see dark blotches of dirt on his bed. "It was a dream … wasn't it?"

The shotgun fired.

Something struck the cabin wall with the weight of a two-ton truck. Glass shattered.

"What was that?" Angie asked, frightened.

Before I could answer I heard Hugin just outside our window, growling low and hard as if he had a grip on some animal that he wouldn't let go. Grandpa screamed. Hugin struggled, roaring and growling. Then he made a *yipping,* almost human cry of pain.

An object hit the house. Smaller than the first time.

The shotgun fired again.

"What's going on?" Michael asked.

I was trying to sit up. Unsuccessfully. "I don't know. But I have to find — "

I was cut off by a scream.

Grandpa was crying out, a long and painful wail that suddenly died. This was followed by a roar I knew wasn't a dog or a man.

I found I could move. I grabbed for the key to the door, knocking it to the floor.

I saw Michael stand up. He struggled to take the few steps to the window.

"Don't!" I yelled.

He looked at me.

"You don't know what's out there," I said, then I scooped up the key and went to the door. "We … we need to arm ourselves. We need something to protect us."

It took a moment of fumbling to place the key in the lock. Then it wouldn't budge. "Oh no … Oh no," I whispered.

I twisted and twisted.

With a clicking sound the key turned. I quickly rotated the knob and threw open the door.

Michael and Angie followed me into the darkened living room.

"What's out there?" Michael asked. "Was it a bear? Did you see it?"

"No," I answered. "But I think whatever — whoever — it is, it's really big."

I found it hard to move. My body was still clumsy. My legs and arms were tingling.

Michael went to the closet and found a bat. I took the hockey stick that was above the mantel and gave a steel poker to Angie. The stick felt too small in my hands. Who'd be scared of me?

We went to the back door, stopped, and looked at each other. I breathed in, my first good breath of air. "Let's do it," I said.

Michael turned the knob.

11

There was one light in the back yard, high on a pole. It seemed to have only about 40 watts of power, just enough brightness to turn everything into shadows. We took a few tentative steps outside. What I saw was enough to frighten me.

A large section of the fence was broken; long, thick slabs of wood looked as if they had been snapped like toothpicks. Grass was uprooted all across the yard. Then I looked to my left. Part of the cabin was caved in, boards stuck out like broken bones. It was the spare room — where we had slept. And it looked like there was blood on the wall. A large, spattered, black pool.

"It's a battlefield!" Michael exclaimed. "What happened?"

"I don't know. But we have to find Grandpa." I clutched my hockey stick tighter and started out into the yard.

"Grandpa! Grandpa!" we yelled.

It was hard to make sense of the shapes around me. There was too much gloom and darkness. I squinted, wondering if I should take the time to find a flashlight. There had to be one in the house somewhere. But what if Grandpa was just a few feet away, lying on the ground?

I stumbled across a groove in Grandfather's tiny garden. It was as if something had been dragged along the earth, through the carrots and pea plants. Part of Grandpa's plaid shirt was stuck to a rake.

I picked up the tattered cloth. It was stained with a dark wet spot. I wasn't sure if it was blood.

My heart sped up. I followed the track, coming closer to the end of the yard.

A few steps later I found his shotgun. The double barrel was bent upwards.

Then I came to the edge of the fence. Boards and posts and wire were all broken and snapped, pointing inward, like a bulldozer had slammed through it all. Just past that were trees and underbrush.

I thought I could hear a rustling sound.

"Grandpa?" I whispered. I couldn't take another step. I felt safe in the yard, in the dim light. "Grandpa?"

The bushes moved. A twig snapped.

I moved backward. Could I hear breathing? Deep, animal-like inhalations?

"Do you see something?" Michael asked.

It took me a second to find my voice. "Y-yes. We better call the police."

I was still stepping backward but looking ahead. Finally I turned and started running quickly towards the cabin.

Angie and Michael followed.

Michael slammed the door behind us and put his weight against it.

Angie was standing behind him, her hands tight on her steel poker. "Phone the cops!" she yelled. "Phone the cops!"

I dialed 911, hoping emergency numbers were the same in Canada as they were at home. An operator answered and I quickly told her what had happened, trying not to sound panicked. I must have spoken too fast because she commanded me to calm down and repeat everything slowly, which I did. "Make sure you stay in the house," she said before she hung up.

Michael was staring out the door's window. "I don't see anything," he said. "Do you know what you saw?"

"I … I didn't really see anything. I just … thought I heard breathing." I paused. "I could just feel it there … looking at me."

"Maybe it was Grandpa," Angie suggested.

"No. It was like an animal or something."

I went to the living room window. The yard was still.

"Oh … jeez," Michael exclaimed.

"What?" I asked.

He was gawking down at his sleeve. There was a small gash on his upper right arm. "I must have cut myself. Not too deep but it's bleeding."

I stayed at the back door while Angie helped him wash the wound and wrapped a handkerchief around it. I noticed Michael was limping when he returned.

A few minutes later I could hear a siren. We went out the front door and huddled together on the driveway, holding our weapons. We looked like rejects from some sports team.

I imagined lights flicking on and people looking out their windows as the cop car zoomed past. The whole neighborhood was probably waking up.

A police cruiser turned into the driveway and came skidding to a halt on the gravel. The siren stopped, but they left the flashing lights on. Two officers got out at the same time, both tall, wearing dark uniforms.

The driver introduced himself. "I'm Lieutenant Roberts." He said *leftenant* instead of *lewtenant*. He had a mustache and serious dark eyes. "Is the intruder still here?"

"No," Michael said. "At least we don't think so."

Then I explained quickly what had happened, adding that I thought I heard an animal just outside the fence.

"Show me to the back yard," Roberts commanded.

They followed us through the house and outside again. Lieutenant Roberts and his partner looked around with their flashlights.

The other officer pointed his light at the wall. It *was* a splash of blood. He moved a few steps closer and examined it. "There's pellet shots here from a shotgun," he said.

Lieutenant Roberts was walking around shining his flashlight in different areas of the yard. He bent over and eyeballed the shotgun. Then he walked to the edge of the fence. I watched, holding my breath, wanting to tell him not to go too far.

He stepped past the fence line. Into the underbrush. He was shining his light there.

"Oh dear," he said suddenly. "Oh no."

Something in the tone of his voice frightened me. I had to see what he was looking at. I took a few steps towards him. He was pointing his light on a pile of grass and upturned dirt. I glimpsed a gray shape — but it seemed so far away — it looked like the mangled form of an animal.

A dog. Hugin. Legs and head at crazy angles.

Was it his breathing I had heard?

Lieutenant Roberts pointed the flashlight back at us. Blinding me. "Sandowski, you better radio for backup. We'll need some search equipment and a few more pairs of eyes. And get those kids inside."

Officer Sandowski led us into the house and got us to sit down. "Don't move, please," he said. Angie was shaking, so he picked up a blanket and gave it to her. Then he went out to the car.

None of us spoke. I couldn't even think straight anymore.

A moment later Sandowski returned. "Do you three have anyplace you can stay tonight? Any other relatives close by?"

"No," Michael answered. "We just know Grandpa. We're here for a holiday."

"Well, I'll have to arrange for someone to come — "

There was a sudden loud knock at the door.

He turned, confused. He went to the front door and opened it, his hand on his holster.

Althea, the woman from the bookstore, was standing there.

12

"I will look after them," she said. Althea stepped past the officer and into the house. She was wrapped up in a thick, gray shawl. She seemed to be glaring with her one good eye.

Sandowski stepped back. "But … Mrs. Thorhall. Did they phone you? I don't understand. How did you know to come here?"

"I heard you go past my house. I live a little less than a mile away. I knew something bad had happened. Thursten asked me to take care of the children if anything went wrong." She turned towards us, squinting. "Are all of you alright?"

I nodded. So did Michael and Angie.

"Did Mr. Asmundson expect trouble?" Sandowski asked.

"He said he saw a large animal earlier this afternoon. He thought that it might be a bear. He borrowed my dog to help him track it."

"I don't think a bear could make that much …" He paused, looked at us then back at Althea. "Anything you could tell me would help."

"Why don't we go in the yard for a second?" Althea suggested. "You three sit tight."

Althea and the officer went out the back door. I could hear

her talking to him, but none of the words were loud enough to comprehend. A third voice joined in: Lieutenant Roberts.

"What's going on?" Angie asked. "Does she know something?"

I shrugged. "If she does, she doesn't want us to hear it."

A moment later I heard Althea say, *"Oh no ... oh no ... no ... not him."*

I realized they had probably told her about Hugin. There was a long period of silence, then they began talking again.

"We're being left in the dark," Michael said. "Just because we're kids."

The door opened. Althea came in, both officers a step behind. "That's all I really know. If you need any help, please call me."

"We will," Lieutenant Roberts promised.

Althea gathered her shawl tighter around her shoulders. "All that's important is to get the children out of this house ... now. To let you do your work."

"Yes," he agreed. "If you can take them that would be a big help."

Althea turned to us. "I know this is all a little rushed, but please grab your clothes and come with me. Your grandfather phoned me earlier and asked me to look after you. Apparently you have a bus to catch tomorrow morning."

"I'm not going on that bus," Michael said.

Althea looked at him, calmly. "I understand. We can talk about that in the morning. Everything will make a lot more sense then. Please, we must go."

Something in the tone of her voice made me believe her, made me hurry. I went to the bathroom and changed into jeans and a sweatshirt. A few minutes later we were at the door, ready to go, our suitcases in hand.

Lieutenant Roberts was there. "Your grandfather will be

just fine," he promised. He didn't seem to believe what he was saying — he was just repeating a line he had practiced again and again in some police drill.

"I hope so," I answered.

We followed Althea to her green truck, walking in a dream. It was a big old monster of a vehicle with an extended cab. Michael had to tug pretty hard to open the passenger door. We slid in silently.

Everything was happening too fast. I wanted to somehow slow it all down so that my thoughts could catch up.

"Close the door tight," Althea said.

Michael slammed the door and a moment later we were on the dark road, dim lights shining ahead of us. Two police cruisers passed by, heading towards Grandpa's cabin.

I almost started crying.

"It's all going to work out," Althea said, she touched my shoulder. I glanced at her. The dash lights cast dark shadows in her wrinkles, making her look even older.

I couldn't think of anything to say, so I just stared down. We traveled the rest of the way in silence. Soon she pulled up to her house, an old, white, two-story building with a bright yard light.

We all got out and followed her inside. Her home was warm and inviting.

"Would you like anything?" she asked. "Tea? Hot chocolate?"

We shook our heads. I was too tired to even yawn. I glanced at Michael and Angie. They could barely keep their eyes open. "I think we just need to sleep," I said.

Althea showed us to our room on the second floor. Two beds covered with huge quilts. A small window. An old radiator in the corner. It felt cozy and safe.

Althea said goodnight and we slipped into our beds. I

wanted to say something to the others … even goodnight
… but I was just too exhausted. Too much had happened
and my body felt heavy.

The quilts were warm and thick.

I fell asleep.

13

I woke up to bright morning light streaming into the bedroom and to the smell of bacon. A moment later Althea knocked gently on our door.

"Good morning," she said. "Breakfast is ready."

I mumbled thanks, slid out of bed, and gathered up my clothes.

"It just doesn't seem real," Angie said.

"What doesn't?"

"This room. All the sunlight. It's like nothing happened last night. Like it was all a dream."

Michael gently removed the handkerchief on his arm. The wound was thin and dark. "Everything happened all right. My arm hurts and my leg feels like it was squeezed in a pair of vise grips." He lifted the leg of his pajamas. A purple, circular bruise colored his ankle. "I really would like to know how that happened."

I thought I knew, but I kept my mouth shut. It just seemed too early in the morning to start thinking about things like that. I went to the bathroom and changed into jeans and a T-shirt. It's funny, my ankle seemed to hurt too. I looked at it, but there was nothing wrong. I guess I was just feeling sympathy pains for Michael.

I needed to have a bath. There was a huge bathtub in one corner, with legs shaped like tiger's paws. It would be so nice to take a long soak, to get all the stiffness out of my muscles. But I didn't have time.

I wandered downstairs, following the smell of bacon and coffee to the kitchen. I passed through a hallway and stopped in the living room. There were hundreds of books on a bookshelf that went from the floor to the ceiling, all neatly stacked and ancient looking. No Danielle Steele or Stephen King books here. Most of them were in other languages, Old Icelandic I guessed — with names like *Volsunga Saga* and *Ari's Libellus Islandorum*. I touched the jacket of one of them and tiny pieces came off on my fingers. I wouldn't have been surprised if some of these books were the only copies in the world.

Three books lay open on the coffee table.

What would Althea be reading?

I heard the clinking of cutlery in the kitchen, she was obviously busy. I padded over to the table and looked at the first one. It was as aged as all the others, a book that looked like it had been brought over here on a Viking ship and carried across the land in a treasure chest.

It was open to a dark, ink drawing of a huge man in a tattered tunic with a fur vest. His arms were bare and bulging with muscles. He was kneeling on a giant, ugly, black shape that could barely be called human looking. He seemed to be holding the creature down. The thing's eyes were glowing in a frightening way. And the moon was shining on them both.

Not exactly what I wanted to see first thing in the morning.

I carefully turned the book over, afraid it would fall apart, and saw that it was titled *Grettis Saga*. It was the story of Grettir, the man whom Althea said was our ancestor.

I set it down. I glanced at the other two books and realized they were journals. I peered at the writing inside the one on top. It was all scribbled, written by someone in a hurry.

The smell of bacon finally drew me towards the kitchen.

"Sarah, you're up!" Althea was standing by the stove, scraping a huge pile of scrambled eggs from a black iron pan into a bowl. She was wearing a dark brown dress that reminded me of an oversized potato sack. Except it looked really comfortable. "I thought I'd have to bang on your door with a hammer." She smiled and winked with her good eye.

"Uh … no you wouldn't have to do —" I started and before I could say anything else, Michael and Angie stumbled into the room behind me, rubbing the sleep out of their eyes.

"You're all awake. Good." Althea was still smiling, though I noticed now that she looked tired and strained, like she hadn't slept for ages. Had she been reading all through the night?

"Did you hear anything about Grandpa?" Michael asked.

Althea nodded. "I talked to the police this morning. They … they haven't found him yet. They're going to continue looking today. They're organizing a search party."

"Do they know what … who he was fighting with?" I asked.

"No," Althea answered. "But they probably didn't tell me everything. That's the way the police do things."

"What can we do to help?" Angie's voice sounded as worried as I felt.

"I don't think you can really do very much. I'm sorry but that's the truth. It's in the hands of the RCMP now — they'll take care of everything." She came over with a plate of fluffy yellow scrambled eggs and bacon. "I know this is bad for your arteries, but eat up. You have a long day ahead of you."

We ate. And despite my mood, the food tasted delicious. The bacon crispy and perfect. I followed it all with a small glass of orange juice. When we were finished, Althea looked at us. "Just leave the dishes. I'll get them later. You better hurry, we have to get to the bus depot in the next hour. The bus leaves at 10 AM sharp. And they don't wait for anyone."

"We can't go," Michael said.

Althea looked down. She spoke softly, her voice persuasive. "I understand, Michael. You're worried about your grandfather. That's only natural. But what do you expect to do? Help the police? They know what they're doing. It will be better if you three go home, to your parents."

"And wait?" I asked.

"Yes. Wait. That's all we can do now," she answered.

"But — " Michael started.

Althea still spoke softly. "No, Michael. I promised your grandfather I would send you home. That's what I intend to do. You'll be safer there."

"Safer?" I asked. "What do you — "

Althea shook her head. "It will be better for you, is what I meant. Better for all of you. Now, please, go and get ready. I'll take you into town in twenty minutes."

We left the table and went to our room.

"This is stupid," Michael said as he zipped his overnight bag closed. "We can't just leave Grandpa here. Not without knowing what happened to him."

"We don't really have much choice," Angie said. "Grandpa wanted us to go home. Althea wants us to go. What can we do?"

I sat on the bed. "It just seems like something's going on and no one's explaining it to us because they don't think we can handle it."

"I agree," Michael said. "Althea and Grandpa are both

keeping secrets."

I was starting to feel a little angry. "We have to find — "

"Are you ready?" Althea asked through the half-open door. I nearly jumped out of my skin. I hadn't heard her come upstairs. "I have the dishes done and the truck running."

"Uh …" Michael paused. "Uh … yeah."

The door swung open. She was smiling. "Then come on. Let's pile in and head to town." Her voice had that fake cheeriness that sometimes crept into my parents' voices when they were trying to get me to do something I didn't want to do.

We followed her downstairs and out into the driveway. It was a warm, perfect day, already starting to get a little hot. All across Gimli, families would be heading out their doors to go suntanning and boating. But we were on our way to a bus and home.

We got into the truck. Michael sat in the tiny seat in the back. Althea looked around, left then right, as if she was afraid of running over something. Then she sighed and I thought I could hear real sadness in her voice. I glanced at her.

"I was looking for Hugin," she explained. "He usually comes with me when I go to town."

She took a deep breath and put the truck in reverse, turned around, and headed out onto the paved road. She went left, away from Grandpa's cabin and towards town. She drove slowly.

Somewhere behind us in the trees there were police officers calling for Grandpa, looking for prints, their German Shepherds following scent trails that no one else could see. Would they find anything?

I didn't think so. I just knew it in my gut.

We drove on. After a few minutes I remembered what I

had discovered in the living room. "Althea?"

"Yes?" she answered.

"I — I noticed some books in your study. This morning. One of them was Grettir's Saga."

"Oh, yes. I was reading it last night."

"It was open to a battle scene. Is that where Grettir fights that … that …" what was the word Grandpa used? "… *thrall?*"

"You know about Grettir and Glam?"

"Yes."

"That's the point where Grettir is cursed by Glam. He says he will always see Glam's glowing eyes before him, whenever it is dark or he is alone. So he will never be at peace."

"Why were you reading it last night?" I asked sharply.

"I …" She paused. "I was reading it because after I met you in my store, it reminded me that it had been a long time since I'd looked it over."

"Oh," I said. I wasn't sure why I had asked her. "What were the other books?"

"You're certainly inquisitive, aren't you? Your grandpa said you were pretty sharp." She glanced at me, smiling slightly, then looked back at the road. "They were old family histories. Just reading about my relatives and such. Nothing more than that."

I nodded. I wanted to ask her another question, but couldn't think of anything that didn't sound stupid. I was missing something somewhere.

We passed the sign that said: "Gimli 1 kilometre." The morning sun erased all the shadows and seemed to have polished up the town, making it look clean and perfect.

A short while later we pulled up at the bus depot. Two cars and a pickup truck were parked in front. There was a coffee shop right there and a laundromat. Neither seemed very busy. A Grey Goose bus sped past us, momentarily blocking the sunlight.

"Is this where we catch the bus?" Angie asked once we had parked. "It looks different in the day."

"This is it." Althea opened her door. "I'll go inside and get your tickets. It's plenty hot out, so why don't you three have a seat over there?" She pointed at a bench next to the depot. "The bus should be here in about ten minutes."

We got out of the truck, our suitcases and overnight bags in hand. My luggage felt like someone had stuffed twenty bricks inside. We trudged over and collapsed onto the bench. Althea disappeared into the station. The door squealed as it closed.

"This sucks," Michael announced. "It's just completely wrong."

I agreed with him. But I had no will to move or to say anything else. I felt sapped of my strength. Empty and tired.

A hot dry wind came up, twirling with dust and scraps of paper. It twisted its way against the side of the building and right over us and seemed to hover there. I coughed, rubbed at my eyes. A second later the mini-tornado was gone, but I was still trying to clear my throat. A pound of dirt had found its way onto my face and into my hair.

I heard the door squeak open again.

"Are you alright?" Althea asked. Her voice sounded muffled. Were my ears filled with dust? She had three tickets in her hand. "You sound like you have something stuck in your throat."

"The … wind," I answered. Then coughed again before I could say anymore.

"Maybe I'll get you all a drink before you go." She turned and went back into the depot.

At the same moment I heard a screeching, scraping noise that sounded like metal being twisted and torn in two. The bus was here, slamming on its brakes, bringing another cloud of dust with it. My coughing doubled. The bus went by only a few feet away from us and I glimpsed tinted windows and a bus driver with sunglasses. I knew already that I was doomed to sit beside the most boring person in North America and listen to his or her stories about what it was like to be a kid.

For hours on end.

I stood, choking now.

"Sarah?" Angie asked. "You gonna be okay?"

"No …" I mumbled. The dirt was clinging to the inside of my throat. "Just gonna go … to the bathroom. Wash my face. Gargle water too."

I stumbled away from the bench and into the coffee shop. I pushed open the door into the ladies room. There I twisted on the taps and wet my face with cold water. Then I bent down and gulped a few mouthfuls of icy, bland-tasting water. It woke me up and my coughing slowly died. I ripped off a paper towel and dabbed at the excess water. It was like drying my face with sandpaper.

When I looked in the mirror, I almost scared myself. My hair was wild. There were black bags hanging below my eyes. The stress of the night before had worn lines in my face, deep creases. I looked like one of those old rock stars who should have settled down years ago. Was my face going to stay this way?

But there was something else I hadn't seen before in any of my family pictures. A hardness. A strength. It was revealed in the shape of my jaw, in the steadiness of my eyes — a look that reminded me of my grandfather. A similarity. Passed down through the ages.

Blood of my blood. That's what he was. And he was in danger … a danger I was beginning to realize even the police couldn't save him from.

I drew in my breath. Straightened my back, heard it crack.

I looked around, not sure why — like there was something in the bathroom that I needed to find.

The window was set low in the wall, open to let in the summer air. I went over to it, yanked it all the way up. I knew I could fit through if I stood on the toilet.

And if I went out the front, Althea would see me.

I climbed on the back of the toilet, stood, and pulled myself out. I scraped my knee on some metal part of the window, but didn't really feel it. Then I lowered myself onto the ground and glanced around. I was at the back of the bus depot. Gimli was in front of me. Houses and more houses.

It was only a short dash to the alley. Beyond that was a park.

I was overcome by a burst of new energy. I was taking action, doing something.

I started running.

» 14 «

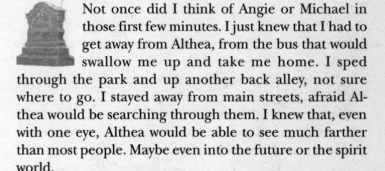Not once did I think of Angie or Michael in those first few minutes. I just knew that I had to get away from Althea, from the bus that would swallow me up and take me home. I sped through the park and up another back alley, not sure where to go. I stayed away from main streets, afraid Althea would be searching through them. I knew that, even with one eye, Althea would be able to see much farther than most people. Maybe even into the future or the spirit world.

I realized that by running I would attract the townspeople's attention, so I slowed to a quick walk. I must have gone down every back alley in Gimli. Finally I found a brick school that was large enough to be a fortress. It seemed quite old, maybe even as old as Grandpa. It was surrounded by a big yard and walled in by a carefully trimmed hedge. I wandered around back and found a hiding place in the bushes. I had this fear that Althea could sense where I was, just like those people who point and find water, so I snuggled deeper into the branches.

I had no idea what I was going to do next or where I would go — just that I had to stay here in Gimli. I hugged my knees. Some of the strength I felt only an hour or two ago was slipping away now that I had stopped moving.

What could I do here? What had happened to Grandpa? I felt small and too young to be trying to do something on my own. And most of all, I felt alone.

Right at this moment, Angie and Michael were riding a bus, miles from Gimli, wondering what had happened to me. I probably should have told them, but I couldn't without getting caught. They'd just have to tell Mom and Dad: "We had a great time, but we lost Sarah. Is that okay?"

A group of crows landed in the grass a few yards away. They pecked at the ground. One of them watched me, showing no interest in worms or bits of garbage at all.

Was every animal in Gimli extraordinarily intelligent?

Grandpa used to say crows were the smartest of all birds and they watched everything and reported back to their master, one-eyed Odin.

Maybe they would lead one-eyed Althea to me. I grabbed a few pebbles and tossed them at the birds. They all took off, cawing and flapping their wings.

Except the largest one. He continued to stare at me.

"Go away," I whispered. "Go back to your nest."

He *cawed*. A loud, startling cry.

"Beat it! Go on!"

He made three more loud *caws*, then with a majestic movement, unfurled his wings. He was even larger than I had first thought. With the easiest of motions he was suddenly in the air. He circled around the bushes three times, then flew off.

Grandpa had also told me that crows were messengers. That often they brought tidings from loved ones.

Was it trying to pass on a message about Grandpa to me?

I shook my head. *Sarah. Sarah. Sarah. This town is getting to you. Now you're starting to think like them.*

I sat for at least another hour, then finally decided it was time to wander again. I got up, dusted myself off, walked out of the school yard, and headed downtown.

I intentionally stayed away from the bookstore. I meandered quickly up and down the streets, not sure what I hoped to find. Finally I saw a sign that said *Ye Ol' Ice Cream Shoppe.* Luckily I had my wallet in my pocket.

I knew exactly what I should do.

I went inside the air-conditioned store. It was small. The whole counter was see-through glass with pail after pail of multicolored ice cream behind it.

"Hello there," an old man said. He had a white cap on and his shirt was like a hockey referee's. It said *Mr. Scoop* on the front. "What flavor can I do for you today?"

I shrugged. Looked through the glass.

"There are so many choices." It was ice cream heaven.

"I'd recommend Tiger, Tiger," he said. "It's the perfect taste for this kind of day."

Immediately I started to salivate. I hadn't eaten anything for hours. "Yes, please. Just a small cone."

He grabbed a cone and started scooping up the ice cream. When he was finished he stood and handed a heaping orange-and-black mass of Tiger, Tiger to me.

"That's as small as we go here," he explained.

I smiled and slid a dollar coin and two quarters over to him. I licked the cone. It tasted perfect. "Uh ... is ... Brand around?"

"Brand?" He raised one eyebrow and winked at me. I didn't get the joke. "Brand's just finishing up in the back."

As if on cue, Brand came out. "All done," he announced. Then he looked at me, smiled. "Hey ... hi! It's Sarah, right?"

"Yes. I ..." I paused. Was I blushing? "I came to take you

up on your offer … to … uh … show me around."

"Good." He waved at the man. "See you, Scoop."

We went outside, down the sidewalk.

"You know," he said softly, "I heard about your grandfather. I just want to say I hope he's okay."

"Me too," I answered. "How did you hear?"

"My best friend's dad is on the force. Derrick Roberts."

"Oh … Lieutenant Roberts … I met him." I paused. "Did your friend know anything about what's going on?"

"Just that they were still looking. That's all he told me."

We walked a little ways in silence.

"He's a tough old guy," Brand said, "He'll pull through."

I nodded, but I couldn't take comfort in his words. Because something had entered my room last night that I had never seen or felt before. If it could tear holes in the cabin and kill Hugin like snapping a toothpick, what chance did Grandpa have? I shivered.

Brand pointed at a long narrow street to our right. "Why don't we walk up this way — we can see the lake then. Boardwalk is just up here."

"Sure."

We changed direction. I finished the last of my cone. The center of my stomach felt cold, as if the ice cream refused to melt.

"So where are your two friends?" Brand asked.

"Uh … Michael and Sarah went home. They had to get back to do some … stuff. They're not my friends though … Michael's my brother and Sarah's my cousin. But I like them just as much as friends. Most of the time, that is."

"I thought you all looked alike, especially you and Michael."

"He's my *tvinnr*."

"Your what?"

I shook my head. Why was I suddenly speaking another language? "My twin, sorry. *Tvinnr* is an Old Icelandic word that Grandpa says is the origin of the English word twin. But yeah, we're twins. Not identical twins, of course."

"Twins! That's cool! You guys ever have any of those twin things happen? You know, he stubs his toe and your toe feels sore … that kind of thing?"

"Well … I'm not sure," I answered. My right ankle suddenly tingled with pain — the same ankle Michael had hurt. Could there be a connection? I wondered.

Brand was staring at me. I blushed. "Uh … sometimes I know when he's just about to make a bad joke."

"I guess that's the same thing." Brand paused. "So you're here by yourself then. Where are you staying?"

"Um …" For some reason I didn't want to mention Althea's name, almost as if she might hear me and come running. "At a woman's place. A friend of Grandpa's. Andrea."

"Andrea who?"

"I can't remember her last name. She lives just past Grandpa's house."

"East, West, North, or South?"

"I'm not sure."

Brand nodded. He was staring at me, almost as if he didn't believe anything I was saying. "I thought I knew most everyone up that way. I guess I don't."

"I think she just moved into her house recently." Now I was outright lying to him. I had to change the topic. "How far is it to the lake?"

"We're almost there." A few steps later he cleared his throat as if getting ready to say something important. Was he going to call me an out-and-out liar? He turned to me, a worried look on his face. "You know … I don't want you to take this in a mean way but … you look really bad."

I had a sudden flash image of how I had appeared in the bathroom mirror, hair pointing in all directions. I didn't imagine I had gotten any prettier, though. I wanted to be at my best around him. "It's … I've been through a lot … that's all."

"Well, we don't have to walk any farther … we can just go sit somewhere."

"I — I actually don't mind walking. It'll help keep me awake. And … uh … I like talking to you too."

He smiled. A very handsome smile. A moment later we went past the last building. We were on Gimli's boardwalk and the lake now appeared in front of us. Brand spread out his arms, sounding like a circus announcer, "Here's the wonderful wacky world of Lake Winnipeg." There were a few motorboats out, one or two sailboats. Seagulls were darting through the air. I suddenly realized that even though my life had been turned upside down and inside out, the rest of the world carried on as it always had.

There were a few clouds forming in the distance. But here we were splashed with bright, warm sunlight. I still felt cold though, as if nothing could heat up my bones after the night before.

"I spend a lot of time here in the summer," Brand was saying. "Water-skiing and fishing and stuff. Have you ever tried tubing? You know — where they drag a tire tube behind a boat. Do they have that in the States?"

"Yes, of course! But I haven't tried it yet."

He smiled. Ran a hand through his short hair. "It's absolutely wild."

We went a bit farther down the walkway. Brand waved at some kids our age out on a motorboat, and they waved back, then made a sharp turn, sending a huge wave rolling our way. I could hear them hooting with joy. That was the kind of fun I wanted to be having right now.

"This lake is huge," I said.

Brand nodded. "I know. My grandma and grandpa used to bring me out here when I was a kid and tell me stories about the lake. It was even bigger during the ice age; it covered most of this part of the province … it was called Lake Agassiz or something like that. Kinda makes you realize how old this place is."

We walked by a giant statue of a Viking. I couldn't help thinking of all the Icelandic people who had settled here. Including my ancestors. I could use their strength and help right now.

"Are your grandparents still around?" I asked.

"Uh … Grandpa died last year. But Grandma's still here. The only person I know who could tell stories as good or better was your grandpa — is something wrong, Sarah?"

"I …" I held my stomach. "I just feel sick suddenly." I knew what it was — just mentioning Grandpa was affecting me. Making my stomach turn with fright.

Then a second wave of nausea swept over me and I felt as if I would black out. The bright sky disappeared, the clouds swirled around me. I knew I was hallucinating. I was buried in dirt and I couldn't move my limbs. I smelled smoke and for one brief moment a face hung in front of me, with a twisted mouth and large, moon-colored eyes. Then I heard a pounding sound, the creaking of wood. A snap.

A moment later it all disappeared. The sky was blue. Brand was saying something I couldn't understand and my knees were shaking.

"Can … can we sit down?" I asked.

He helped me to a bench and we sat. I breathed in and out slowly, trying to steady myself. Finally my stomach returned to normal.

"What was that all about? Your eyes rolled back into your head. I thought you were going to pass out."

"I just got a very powerful feeling of Grandpa. He's in trouble."

"What do you mean?"

"I … I don't know. Just a gut feeling, I guess. Like Grandpa was buried or something."

"Really?"

"Yes … really." I decided it was time for me to take a chance. "Uh … have you ever noticed how … weird this town is?"

Brand laughed. "Weird? Of course, it's what makes us such a great tourist attraction."

"I mean really weird. Scary weird."

He looked suddenly serious. "What do you mean? Did something happen?"

Then I just started talking, not caring if he thought I was some crazy American girl. I described the little boy in the trees and explained how something had broken the window in the cabin. I spoke until I was tired, describing as much as I could. Brand stared seriously at me through all of this, his jaw muscles clenched.

When I was finished he took my arm. "C'mon," he said.

"Where to? The loony bin?"

"No," he said. "I know what we have to do."

15

Brand wouldn't tell me where we were going. He led me back into town and I followed him like a zombie.

He pulled me into an old restaurant with a jukebox and black-and-white pictures of hot rod cars on the wall. He guided me to a booth and sat on the other side. Before I could even open my mouth to ask him a question, the waitress popped up in front of us as if she had just risen through a trap door. Her blonde hair was in a ponytail — she looked like a character from an Archie Andrews' comic.

"Whattya want?" she asked.

"Coke, please," Brand said.

"Hot chocolate," I answered.

She narrowed her eyes. "Hot chocolate? It's twenty some degrees out there, dear."

"Please," I said.

She smiled. Shrugged. "Sure thing. You kids are into the weirdest stuff these days."

After she left, Brand said, "Just sit here, okay. I'll be back in a second."

"Uh … sure."

He stood up and went outside. I watched him walk past the front of the restaurant. He waved and gave me a quick smile. I leaned closer to the window and twisted my neck to see where he was going. He went a little further down the sidewalk and stopped at a pay phone. What was he doing?

The woman appeared with the hot chocolate. I drank, feeling it heat up my stomach. I took another sip and another.

Brand returned a few minutes later.

"Is it helping?" he asked.

"Is what helping?"

"The hot chocolate? Do you feel any better?"

"Yes." I finished off the rest. "It's a lot better now."

"Do you think you really felt what was happening to your grandpa or was it your imagination?"

I paused. The answer came from deep inside me. "No. For a second I was seeing what he saw. Don't you find that a little crazy?"

Brand shook his head. "No. I … uh … when my grandfather died, I saw his spirit. Just kind of floating in front of me. And he said something, then smiled and was gone."

"What did he say?"

"He told me to get good grades."

"What! You're kidding."

"No. He used to say that to me all the time. He wanted me to become a history professor someday."

"Are you saying that was Grandpa's ghost I saw?"

"No. I just think that we are all connected in some mysterious ways. Especially with our own kin."

"So do you mean Grandpa was sending me a message?" I asked.

Brand sipped from his coke. "Yeah … kind of, I guess. I don't know. This just means he's alright."

"For now," I added, and once I said it I realized Grandpa wouldn't be alright for long. He was in danger.

Something else was bothering me. "Who were you talking to on the phone?"

"The phone?" He paused. "Oh … yeah … there's — "

Just at that moment the door to the cafe swung open. Althea swept in, her face set in grim lines.

" — someone I want you to meet."

Althea pointed at me like she'd just caught a jewel thief. "I've been looking for you, Sarah."

16

"Oh … you two know each other." Brand seemed worried. "You didn't tell me that, Grandma."

"I didn't want you to inform her I was on my way." Althea still looked like she was about to explode. She loomed closer to me. "You shouldn't have run away, Sarah."

"I'm not going home," I said, surprised at the serious tone of my voice. Almost as if someone else were speaking through me.

"Not today, you're not … the bus is gone." She was now right in front of me, glaring down. "But you will tomorrow. I made a promise to your grandfather and I'm going to keep it."

"But — " I started.

"Don't argue with me, Sarah." I knew she wasn't making a request. "You and Brand will come with me now."

I sighed. Everyone was pushing me one way, pulling me another. How much more of this could I take? I left money on the table and we followed Althea. Once outside, Brand turned to me. "I didn't know you knew Grandma. I didn't mean to get you into trouble."

"I'm sorry," I said quickly, "I didn't tell you everything. I should have."

We got into Althea's truck and she started it up. "Where are we going?" I asked.

"Home. Where I can keep a close eye on you. I might even be tempted to tie you up."

It didn't sound like she was joking.

With that Althea was silent and we drove all the way to her home without speaking another word. We pulled into the yard, parked in her driveway, got out, and followed her into the house. "You might as well head straight into the back yard." Althea motioned towards the patio. "Just don't run away."

I walked solemnly through the living room, slid the door open.

Sitting on lawn chairs, in sunglasses, T-shirts, and shorts, were Angie and Michael. Michael sat up when he saw me. "Hey, Sis!"

"What are you guys doing here?"

Michael smiled. "Just wondering if we should be mad at you or not."

"Mad at me, for what?"

"For leaving us at the bus depot," Angie cut in. "For not telling us your getaway plan. Nice cousin you are."

"Well …" I paused. "I'm sorry. It just kinda happened. I really should have somehow told you guys."

Michael shrugged. "It's okay. Once we figured out you were gone Althea changed our tickets to tomorrow, so we get to stay an extra day. Of course we aren't supposed to take a step outside this yard." He paused. "She was a little P.O.'d at you."

"I figured that out." I sat on the edge of a weathered bench.

"She'll get over it," Brand said, settling himself on a lawn chair next to me. "She forgives and forgets pretty fast. It's part of being a grandma."

"I heard that!" Althea was standing at the door, right behind us. I turned. She had a container of iced tea in one hand and several glasses in the other. "I forgive people, Brand. But I've got the memory of an elephant. You should know that by now. Remember when you broke my favorite dish because you thought it would make a great frisbee?"

Brand looked a little sheepish. "Uh ... sorry, Grandma," he said.

"It's alright, I forgive you." She came out and set the container and glasses on the round wooden picnic table. She sat down and stared at us. "I think it's time we all had a little talk."

"About what?" I asked.

"I want you to tell me everything you saw and heard last night. Everything. Even if you think it's strange."

"And ..." I started, not sure if I had the guts to pull it off, "... what do we get in return?"

Althea narrowed her good eye, gave me a piercing look. I stared back. "What do you mean?" she asked after a few moments.

I couldn't hold her stare. I glanced down, then back up at her. "I ... uh ... we want to know what's happening. There are things Grandpa didn't tell us — that you aren't telling us. And we want to know what they are. You can't just keep secrets from us because we're young. We're old enough to handle it."

"She's right," Michael added. "We want the truth."

Althea sat brooding for a moment, then she looked directly at me. "You do have Grettir's blood."

I didn't know exactly what she was talking about, but I nodded as if I understood.

» 98 «

Althea looked me up and down. Then stared at Angie and Michael. "Perhaps I've underestimated you. All of you. Maybe it would have been better if I'd told you the truth from the beginning." She paused for another second. "Alright," she said, "I'll tell you everything I know, and you can deal with the nightmares and the possibilities — it's a deal. But first each of you give me your version of what happened. And don't leave out the smallest detail."

Again we spoke about seeing the little boy in the forest and how he had disappeared. Then we all recounted what we could remember about Grandpa's disappearance. Althea nodded and listened closely, asking very few questions. When we were done she sat back. She seemed to believe every word.

"Were any of you hurt or bruised or touched by this visitor?" she asked.

"Yes," Michael said. He moved his legs, displaying the circular purple bruise around his ankle. It looked even worse than this morning. "I don't remember exactly how this happened, but I know it was last night while I was dreaming."

Althea examined his ankle closely. "It's very deep bruising. Does it hurt?" she asked.

"A little, yes," Michael answered. "It's just kind of numb."

Althea rose slowly and went into the house. We were all silent. I looked around the back yard. There was a garden growing there, corn stalks stood straight and tall. There was also a red truck next to a small shop.

Althea came back a few seconds later with a white plastic jar. She dipped her hand in and pulled out a wad of greenish lotion, then rubbed it around Michael's ankle. Once finished she sat back and tightened the lid on the jar. "How does that feel?"

"Much better." Michael was staring at his ankle, a look of awe on his face. "It's tingling and it feels … alive, I guess."

The bruises already appeared to be fading.

Brand gently touched my shoulder. "You should probably tell her about how cold you've been."

"Cold?" Althea was looking at me. "Is this true?"

"Yes." I shivered. "I just can't seem to warm up. And … I forgot to mention … I … uh … saw an image of Grandpa."

"What kind of image?"

"Well it was more like a feeling that he was buried."

"Hmm," she said. "Hmm. This is all making sense. I should have told you from the beginning. Yes, I should have." She stood up. "Just wait here. There are a few things I want to show all of you."

Then she disappeared into the house.

17

"What's she doing?" Angie asked.

We could hear Althea banging around inside, closing and opening doors, dropping things.

"It sounds like she's remodeling the living room," Michael said.

"My guess is Grandma's setting something up for us." Brand was sipping from his iced tea. "I'm not sure if I want to know what it is."

I sat back. The sun's rays couldn't even warm the top layer of my skin. I wanted to find a parka, a pile of blankets, or a roaring fire, but I knew none of these things would be enough to heat me up.

"We talked to Mom and Dad," Michael said to me.

"What did they say?"

"They want us to get home at once — Angie is supposed to come all the way to Missouri since her parents are still in Europe. Dad was quite upset that we couldn't take another bus today."

"Were they upset about Grandpa too?"

Michael nodded. "Yeah, really shaken up. Mom started crying. Dad was asking me all these questions — and I didn't have any answers. Dad's going to fly out here, but he can't get away until tomorrow."

"Well, why don't we wait till he gets here?"

Michael shook his head. "No. He made me promise I would go home tomorrow. That all of us would go."

I sat back. So we would have to leave in the morning, no doubts about it. Had I run away just to delay something that was going to happen anyway?

"Hey," Michael said suddenly, "did you know Dad speaks Icelandic?"

"A little. I didn't think he knew too much, though."

"He and Althea talked for at least five minutes in Icelandic ... I don't think she wanted us to know what they were talking about."

"Did you understand anything they said?" I asked.

"I heard them mention Thursten once," Angie answered.

"Me too," Michael said, "and another name ... Kormak or something. But other than that it was all noise. I couldn't make any sense of it, other than it sounded serious."

"I'll tell you what it was about." Althea was standing at the door. "But not right now. Come into the house. I have a few things to show you."

I stood up, shaky. I was beginning to feel like I had just finished a marathon. We all made our way through the sliding door into the living room. The coffee table had three old books on it. I recognized them as the ones I had glanced at in the morning. There was also a metal vial and a huge, heavy-looking iron cross. Beside them was a pot of tea and five cups.

"Have a seat," Althea motioned and we sat down. Me on the couch beside Brand. Angie and Michael in separate chairs. I shivered. Now that I was out of the sun, I felt even colder. "All of you should drink some of that tea. Especially you, Sarah. It'll warm you up."

I doubted this. I poured myself a cup, sipped it. It had a sharp taste, a tangy lemony scent. I can't say it was good, but I felt it burst against my tongue, down my throat, and spread throughout my body as if it were entering my bloodstream and heating it up. I took another sip. "It works," I said, astonished.

"Yes. But don't drink more than one cup." Althea was sitting across from all of us, near the tea table. "It'll burn some of your inner energy."

She paused. Moved the cross, held it in her right hand.

"I guess I'll start at the very beginning." Her tone was solemn. She wasn't looking at us, but at the cross. Her face seemed more wrinkled, as if just the act of telling this story was draining her. "I'll start with the death of Eric Bardarson. I remember when it happened … I was in my early twenties. I was one of his teachers at the time. He was in grade two, if I remember correctly, and he was really a gentle, lovable kid. Always dreaming. Always happy. It was a pleasure to teach him.

"It had been a very wet spring. There were heavy snows all winter, and the moment it started to warm up enough to melt, the sky darkened and the rain fell. And it kept pouring for weeks on end, so much rain and cloudy weather you could feel it in your bones. It made everyone upset, less likely to say good morning. Some of the older people just gave up — the winter and a hard spring was too much. Needless to say, we all wanted a break.

"It came somewhere in the middle of May. The sun was out one morning and stayed all day, burning away the water. Everyone wandered outside to look, to laugh, to smile. Some of the kids even wore shorts to school, which was against the rules, but we teachers didn't care.

"When the weekend arrived, the earth was getting dry

and a lot of families headed out along the lake or up to Camp Morton to have picnics and play games and visit all their friends whom they hadn't seen all winter. The Bardarsons were one of these families. But unlike everyone else, they went into the woods. You had to walk a long way to get to Thor's Shoulder, a clearing on a giant hill. You could look down on all of Gimli and see the lake. It really was quite beautiful.

"And I guess they had a wonderful picnic. Besides Eric, the Bardarsons also had a boy and a girl a grade or two ahead of Eric. They spent the whole day with each other. Eating and playing games. They let the kids wander around as long as they didn't go too far.

"When it came time for them to leave, Eric had disappeared. His brother and sister said he was right behind them, but when they turned he was gone. The family frantically searched for him for hours, but there was no trace. It was growing dark so the father sent his wife and children to get help and he stayed there calling out Eric's name. He finally grew tired and leaned against a tree. He lit a fire hoping to attract his son. He said he heard many strange sounds that night, howling and voices, but saw nothing of Eric.

"The next morning, and for days after, the search party tramped around the area. They couldn't even turn up a scrap of clothing. It was decided the heavy rains had softened the earth so much that the boy must have fallen into a bog and smothered to death. Others said wolves may have gotten him, but this seemed unlikely because even wolves leave remains.

"There was only one person who lived in that area — old man Kormak. He had a cabin and he survived by trapping animals for his own food and gathering berries and edible plants from the brush. The police did ask him if he knew anything, but they could make no sense of what he said. The rumor was that all the rain pounding on his cabin had driven him insane. I only saw Kormak three times while he was alive. And each time he looked the same: he was a big-boned man, with wild hair and a thick beard. He wore animal skins with the heads still attached. And he never bathed.

"There were rumors that he had something to do with Eric's disappearance. People also whispered that Kormak liked to spend time at graveyards and such … but no one could prove anything. Finally, the search was given up. Every couple of years there's something in the paper about the boy — it's one of the biggest tragedies to hit Gimli."

Althea paused. She reached slowly down to her cup of tea, grasped it, and took a sip.

"What happened to this Kormak guy?" Angie asked.

Althea set down her cup. "He died about five years later."

"Well," I said, "if this boy and Eric are the same person — then why? I mean, what was he doing out there?"

"Let me begin by saying that I've seen him too."

"You have?" Michael asked.

"Yes." Althea nodded. "About four years ago this summer I was on my way north to a reading by a writer friend of mine. I had agreed to set up a display of his work. It was late and I was driving not too far from where you three were walking. All of a sudden there was this little glowing figure on the road — he just appeared out of nowhere. I slammed on my brakes, swerved to miss him, and he vanished. At the same time I came over the rise of a hill and a deer was in the middle of the highway, staring at me. I would have never been able to stop in time. I got out and looked for the boy but he had disappeared."

"You mean he warned you?" Brand asked.

"Yes. I think so. I don't know exactly how he died, but I

think his spirit is here as an omen of sorts — a good omen. I know Eric is more likely to appear in the early summer — it's near the anniversary of his death. Powerful things happen around the anniversary of anyone's death, sometimes good, sometimes bad. I have met a few other people who've seen him. One was a woman hiker who would have fallen into an old well if he hadn't attracted her attention. I think he's there to try and stop more bad things from happening."

"That's awful," Angie said.

"What do you mean?" I asked.

She looked a little sad. "That this poor boy has to wander around, warning people. Never doing whatever little boys get to do in heaven."

Althea nodded. "It does seem unfair, doesn't it? But we don't know what happens next. I don't think time is the same to him. Maybe he drifts from here to a better place and back. Who knows."

"It doesn't sound like much of an afterlife." Angie was frowning now.

"It's not for us to judge," Althea said finally.

I sat back. "What do you think the boy was warning us about?"

"I can't really say for sure. Just that something bad was going to happen. And obviously it did."

"Was he — " I swallowed. "Was he warning us about a *draugr?*"

Althea laughed, so loudly and forcefully that I was shocked. "Heavens no! Thursten's been filling your head full of stories. I'll tell you what I believe happened last night. It's exactly what I told the police."

18

Althea reached for the largest of the books on the table, a tattered and stained journal. It looked like it had been through the wringer a hundred times over. I remembered that it had scribbled handwriting inside.

Althea opened the cover carefully. "Last winter I found a large, brown package waiting for me at the post office — it was this book. It had been sent to me by members of Kormak's family. They still own the land he dwelled on, and one of them had made the journey to the cabin and found this. They kept it at their home in Iceland for a few years, unopened. Then they heard I was writing a history of Gimli, so they sent it to me. It's Kormak's old journals."

"What does a man who died years ago have to do with Grandpa?" Michael asked.

"I'll get to that. Just give me a second." She flipped through a few pages, read a bit to herself, then flipped ahead some more. All the paper was yellow and the book looked like it would fall apart. "Ah, here's something." She pointed at the page. " '*And I can feel the hatred boil up, a living thing inside me. Every time I see his face, hear his voice ... I know he is my born enemy. I loathed his father ... I loathe him.*

This Thursten from the valley, son of Thorgeir.' Then Kormak writes *dreyri* about twenty times in a row."

"What's that mean?" I asked.

"Blood. He seemed pretty obsessed with blood."

"Was it Grandpa he hated so much?" Angie had her arms crossed.

"Yes," Althea answered. "It was. About the time this was written, your grandfather had just arrived here from the old country. By talking to him and by doing research on my own, I discovered Kormak was one of the Grotsons, a family that had a long-standing grievance with the Asmundsons, your family. He had moved here and brought the feud with him."

"What was the feud over?" I asked.

"Well about seventy years ago, Kormak's father accused your great-grandfather of stealing one of his cows. It even went through the courts and Thorgeir was declared innocent. But there was a rumor that the old farmer actually was in love with your great-grandmother … though she'd never had anything to do with him. Apparently he passed this hatred down to Kormak."

"Did he ever do anything to Grandpa?" Angie asked.

Althea shook her head. "No. Just wrote in this book. Kormak was a little bit bothered in the head. Pretty well everyone whom he had cross words with — and that was a lot of people for a hermit — ended up in this journal. But most of the entries were about Thursten."

"Okay," Michael said, "So this Kormak guy didn't like Grandpa and he wrote a bunch of mean stuff, then he kicked off. What's this have to do with today?"

"Well …" Althea flipped ahead a few pages. "Right here is Kormak's last entry, presumably written only a few hours before he died. It says, '*Revenge will be mine after night, after death, after everything. The light will not claim me.*' It's dated the same day he collapsed in his front yard with a failed heart: June 30th, 1945."

Althea flipped ahead another page or two. "And right here the strangest thing happens. There are new entries written after Kormak's death. With dates sometime in the last five years, if they can be believed."

My heart had skipped a beat. "New entries?"

"Yes, written in a similar hand as before ... but forty-five years later. Here, I'll read you one." She ran her finger down the page, stopped. "'*Darkness and fog and cold creep through my bones. I have had dreams and heard crowing voices, twice now the wolves and rats and all the dark creatures have come knocking at the door. The third time will be the last.*'"

"It doesn't make any sense," Brand said.

"No," Althea answered. "Not at first. But when you read more it starts to make a certain crazy semblance of sense. Here's another one. '*And I feel the hatred wrap around my flesh and sink its fangs into my heart. It is eating at me like the snake Jormungand who bites his own tail. It is an old, old hatred passed down through my flesh, my spirit, my bones — from father to son to son. A hatred for one man, one name: Thursten.*' This entry is dated only three years ago.

"I'll read you the very last one. It's the worst. '*Blood. Dead. Flesh. I am returned from the dirt, up from the ground. Draugr ... Draugr ... Draugr ...*'"

"Did Kormak write this?" I asked.

"No. Kormak was long, long dead and buried. His son wrote it."

"Son?" I had finished the last of my tea and was beginning to feel the coldness creep into my system once again. "His son?"

Althea nodded. "Well, I did a little research on this — I

don't think his family read all the book. They just saw it was old and sent it to me — I'm good friends with Kormak's first cousin. I got the impression they weren't too proud about Kormak's branch of their family tree — but they did find him interesting.

"After I read the journal I wrote to the Grotsons about the new entries. They sent back a letter saying they didn't know anything about them. But they included a piece of information that made me think quite a bit. They said Kormak had married only a year or so before he left for Gimli. His wife was quite young and many believed it was an ill match and that he had somehow bewitched her. Anyway, he left her with child and vanished to Canada. He apparently never saw his first and only offspring — a boy.

"They told me his son was *fúinn* — rotten inside. His mother had a hard time raising him, it took years from her life. Apparently her hair went gray and her skin wrinkled up by the time she was twenty-five. He fought with everyone, was kicked out of school, and spent time in jail. But all this time his mother told him what a great father he'd had. She died, presumably of exhaustion, when she was thirty-four. Some of the relatives tried to care for the boy, but within six months he had disappeared. No one heard about him again for years. He just wandered around Iceland and Norway, wherever he could find trouble."

"What was his name?" Michael asked.

"Kar. About five or six years ago, people who knew of him thought they had seen him passing through Gimli. He looks just like his father, sallow sunken eyes and heavy cheekbones. The people who saw him went to church that night to pray for the town. They said looking into his eyes was like looking into the burning orbs of the Devil."

"A few days later I was down having coffee at a restaurant

and I heard that hunters had seen lights in Kormak's cabin. Of course, no one dared to go near it. Even fifty years later, no one wants to have anything to do with Kormak."

"So you think this Kar wrote in the journal?" I was starting to understand what Althea was getting at.

"Yes, he might have stayed at the cabin and later his family members, not knowing he had lived there or was still there, took this from the table. I think Kar read it, then started to hate your grandfather just like his father did. His side of the Grotson family is known to be a little … mad. And the stories of people coming back from the dead are pretty common in the old land. He probably made himself believe he was actually undead. And he's been planning his revenge for years. This is what I told the police and they're looking for him now."

"But he couldn't have done all the damage to the house," I said, "one man couldn't have."

Althea narrowed her eyes. "I haven't seen the cabin in daylight yet, but I do know that it was dark and all of you were in a state of fear and worry, and sometimes your imagination makes your memories bigger than what you actually saw."

"But — " I started.

"You would also be surprised how much destruction a deranged Icelandic man can do."

I fell silent. I wasn't sure what was right. Maybe it only was a few broken windows and boards magnified by my frightened mind.

"There's one more thing you should know." Althea looked seriously at us all. "Your grandfather and I traced your family lines back. And this Kar is actually related to you — a third cousin."

"We're related to this crazy guy!" Michael exclaimed.

"Great gene pool we come from."

Althea spoke slowly. "This is what I believe happened. You're old enough that I can tell you the truth. I think Kar has probably dragged Thursten away and buried him ... but kept him alive. *Draugrs* were known to do this to their victims as a sort of slow revenge. That means your grandfather is most likely still alive."

"For now," Michael whispered.

We were silent.

"What can we do?" I asked finally.

"Pray," Althea answered. "Tonight — "

The phone buzzed. It was sitting on a small desk and looked like it was a fax machine too.

Althea went to it and picked up the receiver. "Hello."

She paused for a moment. Her face became serious, set in stone.

"I understand. Yes, I will be there shortly."

She set down the phone and turned to face us. "The police are having difficulty locating Kar's cabin. Even their dogs seem to lose their sense of direction. I'm going to go out and help them."

"Why you?" Brand asked, clearly concerned about his grandmother.

"Because I know those woods better than anyone. I'll be safe. There will be six officers with me." She smiled. "It's not every day I get to be around six handsome men in uniform."

A minute later she was at the door, workboots on, her shawl around her shoulders. "Brand, there are leftovers in the fridge. Please, feed our guests." She turned to us, her one gray eye serious. "We will find your grandfather," she promised.

Then she was out the door and gone.

» 19 «

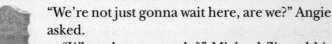 "We're not just gonna wait here, are we?" Angie asked.

"What else can we do?" Michael flipped his hair out of his eyes. "We have to sit right here. But I don't know if I'll be able to stand it."

"Grandma knows what she's doing," Brand said. "She's worked with the police before — she helps them quite a bit. And if anyone can find your grandfather, she can. She has a gift for those kinds of things."

"You mean she's done this before?" I asked.

"No … not exactly," Brand answered. "She just has a knack for finding things, including people. Once when I was a kid I ran away from home and, to make a long story short, I got lost in the dark. For hours. She was the one who found me. She just knew exactly where I was."

"Yeah … you're right," I said. "She seems like she's capable of anything." The noose in my stomach was loosening. I sighed. "The police are trained for this kind of thing too. Everything will work out."

"The Mounties always get their man," Brand said, a little flippantly. He was smiling. "It's what they're known for." He stood up. "You know what we need right now is a little grub. How about leftovers?"

"I'll help," I said a little too quickly. Angie gave me a quick wink. "That is, if you need help."

Brand motioned with his hand. "Sure. The more the merrier." Then he headed for the kitchen.

I ran a hand through my hair and my fingers got stuck in the knots. "I have to go to the washroom first," I said. I turned left and went up the stairs. I thought I could hear Angie and Michael laughing behind me.

Once in the bathroom, I looked in the mirror. There was dirt on my face, my hair looked even worse than it had in the morning. Oh no! My heart sank. I had looked like this all day. I found a brush and quickly brushed out the knots, practically pulling my hair out. When I was done, I pulled it back and tied it with a barrette I found on the counter.

Then I laughed at myself. Here I was worried about my looks on probably one of the worst days of my life. It was silly.

I did take the time to wash my face.

Just before I left I stared at myself.

That hard look I had seen before was still there. A feeling of strength.

I wished I could understand where it was coming from.

I found Brand in the kitchen, opening the oven door. A turkey pie was in his right hand. He slid it into the oven. "This'll be perfect," he said to me. "You got here just in time ... what temp should it be?"

I turned the knob to 375 degrees. "It'll probably take at least twenty minutes."

I glanced up. Brand was staring at me, a look of caring in his eyes. "How are you feeling?" he asked quietly.

"Uh ... good," I answered, suddenly feeling queasy. "Better, I guess, now that I know Althea is going to help in the search."

"All three of you should get medals. You've held up really well." He paused. "In fact, you deserve a medal for getting away from Grandma. I would have thought it impossible."

I smiled. "It already seems like it was years ago."

Brand put his hand on my shoulder and squeezed lightly. "Your grandfather has probably whipped this Kar into shape and is just waiting for the cops to show."

I smiled. "Yeah. I hope so."

Brand opened his mouth to say something else and at that moment the phone buzzed twice. He shrugged, went over, and put the receiver to his ear. Instead of saying hello, he reached down and pressed a button. The phone made a squealing noise, then I heard a humming sound.

"A fax is coming through," Brand explained. "It's probably from one of Grandma's writing friends — they're always faxing each other about Viking myths."

Brand watched the paper come out the top. "Wait a second — " he paused, "it's from the Mounties."

He watched until it was completely printed. Then read it over. "Oh my ..." he whispered.

"What is it?" Michael asked.

Brand looked up, his face suddenly serious. "It's from one of Grandma's friends in the RCMP detachment. Grandma must have asked her to look up the records on Kar. Apparently there was some kind of computer problem, so they couldn't get the information right away. But it says this Kar guy died three years ago. Someone found him dead up in the trees — he had been attacked by an animal of some sort. He was buried in the Gimli cemetery." He paused. "They're going to concentrate on a few other leads. They brought park officials in to help them track a bear."

"A bear?" Michael asked. "Do they believe it's a bear now?"

Brand shrugged. "I don't think they really know."

"Let's go for a drive," I blurted.

"A drive?" Brand looked at me like I'd turned into an alien. "Grandma should be back soon. Besides, I only have my learner's license."

"Where do you want to go?" Michael asked. Was he thinking along the same lines as me? I glanced at him, saw a look of concern.

"Well …" I paused. I suddenly realized how bizarre my idea sounded. I realized I had to say it anyway. "I want to go to the graveyard."

"The graveyard?" Brand exclaimed. "Are you crazy? Why do you want to go there?"

"I just have a hunch that's all. About Kar."

"Which is?"

"I'll know when we get there. That some kind of clue about Grandpa will be waiting at the cemetery."

"I think she's right," Michael said. He still had that same concerned look. "Let's go."

"Yes, let's go," Angie echoed. She too seemed very serious. Was it some kind of family ESP? Did they have the same hunch as me? All three of us had gathered around Brand.

"We can't just go." He took a step back. "I can't drive without an adult."

"We'll be okay as long as you drive safe," Angie said. "Besides, if you add all of our ages together — we're in our thirties."

"Forties, actually," Michael added. "Forty-two to be exact."

Brand took another step back. "But it'll be dark soon."

"We'll take flashlights," I answered. All three of us moved closer.

"You Americans are crazy. Grandma will kill me."

Angie put her hand on his shoulder. "We'll be gone to-morrow. We won't be anymore trouble after that."

Brand paused. He looked at us, shaking his head and grinning. "Oh … okay. You win. If we hurry we can get back before Grandma returns."

We cheered. Michael punched Brand playfully on the shoulder. "It'll be wild."

"It better be. Cause I'll be spending the rest of the summer in the dog house."

Brand went to the broom closet and dug out two huge, black, metal flashlights. They were the kind the police usually carried. I turned the oven off, put the turkey pie back in the fridge. Within a minute we were all ready to go.

Brand handed a flashlight to Angie and one to me. "We can take my grandpa's truck. It's out behind the house. I don't think it's been driven for a couple years, so we might be hoofing our way back."

"Let's hurry," I said. "Please."

Brand looked at me. His face was solemn. "Okay, for you I will."

Then we followed him through the patio doors and into the back yard.

20

The truck was the one I had spotted before — an old red Chevy with big tires, rectangular windows, and curved metal fenders. It gleamed in the sunlight.

"Is this a '57?" Michael asked.

"It sure is," Brand answered. "Grandma said she'd give it to me when I turn sixteen. She'll probably change her mind after tonight."

We piled into the truck and slammed the doors. Brand found the keys under the floormat. "Cross your fingers everyone." He gently pushed the keys into the ignition and pressed in the clutch. "It's been a long, long time since this baby's been started." He turned his hand.

The truck roared to life like it had been waiting years for this one moment. The loud rapping of the mufflers echoed all around us. Brand removed his foot from the gas and it idled evenly. "Well, I'll be damned."

I saw that the gearshift was on the steering column. "Is that a three on a tree shifter?" I asked.

"Yes." Brand gave me a bewildered look. "I'm surprised you know about it."

I shrugged. "One of our neighbors had an old truck like

this. He let me drive it once. For about ten yards. It was weird not to have the shifter on the floor."

"You're full of surprises, Sarah," Brand said. Angie nudged me hard, so that I was sitting right next to Brand. Then she moved over so that I couldn't move back.

I didn't try anyway. I was right against Brand.

Brand pulled the truck into reverse and started backing up. A moment later we were around the front of the house and turning onto the road. "Scream if you see Grandma," Brand said, half serious, half joking.

We turned left, heading for Gimli.

The truck purred along the highway, rumbling melodically. It rode smooth and perfect. Brand drove the speed limit, scanning for potholes and deer.

The setting sun turned the rearview mirror red.

"Hurry, please," I said. I was beginning to get a feeling of urgency. "Hurry!"

"I'm going as fast as I dare," Brand said. "I don't want to attract any attention."

About a mile later we turned off the road and went along the outskirts of town. Shortly after that we pulled up to the Gimli Cemetery. The main gates were made of iron, at least fifteen feet high and set in two pillars. A stone wall surrounded the whole graveyard.

"It looks like a jail," Michael said.

"Yeah," Angie agreed. "It's almost like they don't want anything to get out."

We putted through the gates; the rumbling of the truck was twice as loud here. There was no sign of life, just row after row of headstones, some huge and obviously expensive, others as small as dinner plates.

"I had no idea there'd be so many graves," Angie said. "There are more graves than there are townspeople."

Brand switched the lights to bright. "I wonder where we'll find this Kar's grave? Any ideas?"

"It's only a couple years old," I said, "so it's probably farther back."

We rolled down the road, passing columns of headstones until we were three-quarters of the way through the cemetery.

The sun was falling off the edge of the world. Soon we would have no light at all.

Michael pointed. "That grave was from two years ago."

"Let's stop," I suggested. "We'll have a better chance of finding it on foot. And we might as well split up."

Brand pressed on the brakes, halting the truck. We piled out. Angie turned on her flashlight and she and Michael went one way, Brand and I the other. "Holler if you find the grave," I yelled. "Scream if you see anything weird."

Michael shrieked. It echoed through the graveyard. "Just practicing," he said.

"You're not funny, Michael." Angie pushed him ahead. "Let's get going."

I clicked the light on my flashlight, finding it quite bright. We started walking past headstones. Some for children, some for adults. We were careful not to tread on any graves.

"How will you know it?" Brand asked after a few minutes. "It might not even have a marker."

"I'll know it when I see it," I said with certainty. It was the grave of my grandfather's enemy. All of Kar's anger would still be waiting there, radiating from under the dirt, making the hairs on the back of my neck tingle.

We walked on, keeping a quick careful pace. The lights of Gimli were twinkling to my right but they didn't cast any brightness our way. It seemed we were in a twilight world of dark shapes and gray shadows.

Moments later the world turned completely black. Thick

gray clouds had blotted out the last rays of the sinking sun. My flashlight wasn't very bright anymore. It flickered occasionally and when it worked it cast a dull yellow beam.

"I hope these batteries don't die," I whispered.

"They shouldn't," Brand said. "I've used the flashlight a thousand times. It should work for at least another hour."

I glanced over my shoulder and couldn't see Angie or Michael. "I wonder if they're okay," I worried.

"I'm sure they're fine," Brand answered. "Your brother and Angie seem to be just as capable as you."

I walked on, letting the compliment sink in. He thought I was capable. I'd always felt a little disorganized in my life, like I wasn't doing things right.

He thought I was capable!

"I do wonder," Brand asked, "what exactly you expect to find here?"

"It's … it's just a gut feeling I have. It might be nothing. But I need to look."

"Well, Grandma always says to trust your guts … I thought she was talking about cooking."

I snickered, glad to be able to laugh a little. We continued looking. I flashed my light at stone after stone, reading each name and forgetting it a moment later. Was that all there was to our lives. Would I one day just be a name on a stone, for strangers to pass by?

I felt an icy chill run up my spine.

A dog barked in the distance. Was it barking at us? Or was it a warning?

It stopped after a few seconds.

"Did you get to meet Hugin?" Brand asked.

"Yes."

"Something about that dog just barking there sounded a little like him. It couldn't be, of course … could it?" Brand paused. "He was a really good dog."

"I know. He amazed me."

"My friend overheard his dad talking about how Hugin died. I guess his back was broken and his legs too. And he still crawled after your grandfather, trying to save him." Brand drew in his breath. His face became hard and angry. "I really want to help get whoever did that to Hugin. That's one of the reasons I brought you guys out here. Just in case there is some kind of answer. Something I can do."

I shone my light on the next gravestone. The words were worn by wind and rain, but I could read: *Kormak Grotson. December 6th, 1894 to June 30th, 1945.* "I think there is."

We shuffled closer, careful not to step on the grave. I was afraid my feet would sink down and I would be trapped. Or a hand would come up.

"It's his father's grave," Brand said. "Why didn't I think of that? Kar's final resting place is probably right around here."

"I'll tell the others," I said. I took a step to the side and started to yell, but in that same moment my footing crumbled below me. The flashlight flew from my hand and I found myself tumbling down, down a long slope into wet, dark earth.

I hit something hard and came to a stop.

It took me a moment to regain my senses. There were dark walls of earth all around me and a sore spot on my head. I inhaled a deep breath and smelled the rotten smell of decaying flesh.

I was surrounded by loose dirt. It could fall in at any time.

Panic bubbled up inside me. I pounded away at the ground, feeling trapped.

"Sarah!" Brand called from somewhere above me. "Are you alright?"

"Yes," I said. I stopped flailing. "I've fallen down a hole or something."

I noticed that the flashlight was only a foot away, so I grabbed it and pointed it down.

I saw wet cool earth, broken boards, and tattered pieces of clothing. I was standing on top of a casket.

It was empty.

I caught my breath. I was in a grave.

"Keep cool. Keep cool," I repeated.

"What?" Brand said. "Did you say something?"

I shone the light up. I was only a few feet from the ground. It wasn't that deep after all. I saw Brand's face floating in the air. His hand extended towards me out of darkness.

Then my light hit a small grave marker above me. It read: *Kar Grotson. April 16th, 1942 – June 30th,1993.*

I was standing on Kar's casket.

Suddenly I remembered where I'd smelled the familiar earthy smell. In my room at Grandpa's, the night before. Right after the window was broken.

"Get me up! Get me up!" I yelled. "Now!"

I grabbed Brand's right hand. He held on tightly. With him pulling and me desperately digging into the earth I made it to the top in record time. I lay there for a second, breathing hard.

"You gonna be okay?" Brand was leaning over me.

"I — I think so." I paused. "I want to get out of here, though. Now."

I heard running footsteps, saw a bobbing light. Michael and Angie came up. "What's going on?" Michael asked. "We thought we heard screaming."

By this time I had sat up. "We found his grave."

Michael pointed his light down. "It's empty."

"I know." I stood, looked over the edge.

"Well, where is he?" Angie asked. They peeked down as if afraid something would grab them.

"I don't know," I answered. It took all my will to just glance at the casket again. "But look at the boards. They're pointing upwards as if they were broken from the inside."

21

My own words echoed around us. We stared at the open grave, two flashlights trained on an empty casket and a hole half-filled with wet, loose earth.

On impulse I pointed my light at the gravestone. Then I pointed it at Kormak's.

"It's the same day," I whispered. My knees felt like they would give out.

"What?" Brand asked. He held my arm, steadied me.

"They died on the same day," I said. "June 30th. Different years but the same day."

"Wasn't it June 30th just a few days ago?" Angie asked.

"The day before we arrived," Michael added.

"And didn't Althea say there was something powerful about the anniversary of someone's death?" I asked.

We were silent.

"Let's get out of here," Michael said. "I've seen enough. I don't feel safe any longer."

We raced back to the truck, tripping over stones and flower arrangements. I think we might have even trampled across a few graves, but I didn't care. I just had to get out of there. Once inside the vehicle we slammed the doors shut.

We all tried to catch our breath.

"He … he can't be …" Angie trailed off.

I shrugged, tired. "All I know is what I saw."

Brand started the truck, flicked on the lights. Two beams illuminated an army of headstones. My sense of direction was gone. For a moment I wondered if Brand knew the way out.

I didn't want to get lost here. Not in a place where the dead sleep.

Brand pulled the Chevy into gear, turned left, and headed down the road. "Someone could have dug it up," he said. "Broke the casket. And pulled the boards back towards them."

"Why?" I asked. "What would be in there?"

Brand shrugged. "You never know what people are looking for or why they do things. Specially around here."

We headed through the main gate and onto the highway. I sighed quietly. I would feel a lot better with the graveyard behind us.

No one spoke until we reached Althea's house. The porch light was on, but her truck wasn't there.

"Grandma's not home," Brand said, "that's really weird." He pulled up the front driveway and parked. We piled out and headed into the house.

It was exactly as we had left it.

"It doesn't look like she's been here at all." Brand turned on the light to the living room. "I wonder what's taking so long?"

"Maybe we should phone the police," Angie suggested. "They might know where she is."

"It can't hurt," Brand agreed. "I'm starting to get worried."

He dialed the phone. I went into the living room and

paged through Althea's books, which were still sitting on the coffee table. I stopped at the etching of Glam and Grettir battling each other. I looked at it and I knew the person who had drawn this picture had captured something real.

How could Grettir have beaten a creature as huge and full of hate as Glam? It was impossible. And yet he had done it.

We needed someone like Grettir now.

I touched the metal cross beside the books. It was cold and plain. I lifted it and was surprised at its weight. Then for no reason I could understand, an image appeared in my mind. Of Grandpa on the porch, whittling with his knife. And smiling.

What did it mean?

"They said she didn't show up," I heard Brand say. I set down the cross and wandered back to the main room in a trance. "They said they'd send a cruiser up to where she was supposed to meet them."

Brand's words echoed from wall to wall. The room went in and out of focus. I stepped in front of everyone and they all looked at me.

"We have to go to Grandpa's cabin," I said, holding my head.

Brand's eyes widened. "What! First the graveyard and now the cabin! What for?"

"My grandfather was carving something. I want to see what it was."

"No. No. No." Brand held up his hand like a school crossing guard telling a car to stop. "There are cops everywhere. I can't just go driving again. We got lucky last time."

"Brand — we have to go," I said. I straightened my back, felt taller suddenly. "Believe me. It's the only way to get anything done. We've been waiting for everyone else to solve this. We have to take matters into our own hands."

"She's right," Angie said. Just her words seemed to make me stronger. "We have to see what we can find there."

Brand shook his head. "I don't know what they put in Missouri water, but I don't ever want to drink it." With that he spun around and headed for the door. "C'mon, we might as well get going. Just be ready to spend the night in jail."

We followed him back out to the truck. This time he had a problem starting it, the engine turned over and over. "It just doesn't seem to want to catch," Brand said. He stopped, tried again, and it roared.

A moment later we were on the road, heading to the highway. Brand turned right, his foot heavy on the gas. The tires spun in the dirt and squealed when we hit the pavement. "Oops," Brand said.

"I thought we were trying to avoid getting caught," Michael said.

"We are." Brand patted the dashboard. "I sometimes forget how much power this baby has."

We sped down the highway. The sky was completely black; I couldn't see any stars — even the moon's brightness had been cloaked by trees. It only took a few moments to get to Grandpa's cabin. We pulled up the driveway, parked out front. None of the lights were on, so Brand left the truck running with its headlights flicked to bright.

No one moved. We stared out, safe behind our windshield.

The place looked like it had been deserted for a hundred years. The police had placed yellow plastic ribbon around the cabin, marked with the warning: CRIME SCENE DO NOT ENTER. The bushes around the yard seemed to have moved closer to Grandpa's home. I wondered what could be hiding there?

No one said anything. Finally I grabbed the door handle and pushed the door open. It took all my willpower to step outside.

I took another step or two and was relieved to hear Brand's door open. I led everyone up to the cabin. "Here goes nothing," I said, then I ducked under the ribbon and opened the door. I flicked on the light.

The living room looked like someone had swung a wrecking ball through it. The table and couch were overturned, there were books scattered on the floor beside cushions and drawers. Most of the closet doors were open.

"The police must have been looking for clues," I said.

"I wonder if they have a special task force that cleans up after them?" Michael asked.

Brand picked up an overturned lamp and set it on the floor. "It seems like I've asked you this a couple of times tonight — what are we looking for?"

"I don't know," I answered. "Something that Grandpa was carving or making. I think you'll just know when you see it."

"Could you be more specific?" Michael asked.

"That's all I know," I said. I started searching around the main room, grabbing books and turning over cushions. After a few minutes I realized it didn't seem like the right place to find anything.

I went into the room Michael, Angie and I had shared just the night before. The light wouldn't go on. I could see the remaining curtains moving in the breeze. There were thick pieces of splintered wood on the floor. Shattered glass glittered with moonlight.

In the center of the wall, where the window used to be, was a huge gaping hole. Only part of the frame was still there.

No man could have done that.

Michael and Angie were peering over my shoulder. "I don't remember that much destruction," Michael whispered.

"I do," I said.

"Maybe the cops somehow made it bigger." Angie paused. "Like when they were looking for stuff or something."

I shook my head. "I don't think so." Then I stepped past them and out of the room.

A thought struck me. "Do you remember Grandpa going into the guest room to work on something? I think there was a reason why he had you sleep in the same room as us."

"So we'd be safer?" Michael asked.

"That was one reason. But I don't think he wanted us to see what he was doing."

I went down the hall to the spare room and flicked on the light, surprised that it worked. There was a small bed in one corner, a workbench on the other side, and a number of carving tools on top of a cupboard. A few of Grandpa's wood-burning drawings hung on the wall: a bear, a hawk, and a wolf. They looked so real that their eyes followed me when I moved.

Grandpa had left a book open on the bench. Beside it was a small object. When I got closer I saw that it was a wooden cross. He had been burning symbols into it. In the book there was an image of the cross, drawn in ink. Grandpa had about three quarters of the runes from the picture burnt into the cross. It looked beautiful. Next to the cross was a wineskin with a sticky note on it that said: *do not drink ... consecrated water.*

I looked at the front cover of the book. It was hard and black, but there was no title. The words inside were Icelandic, of course.

"Did you find something?" Michael asked. He, Brand, and Angie had piled in behind me.

"I think so." I showed them the book. They examined it. "Grandpa seemed to be working on this cross, but it doesn't look like he was finished what he wanted to get done."

"Do you think it was to ward something away?" Angie asked.

"Probably. But he had this water too. What was he doing?" I asked.

"Getting ready for something, I'd say." Brand was touching the wineskin. "Is consecrated water the same as holy water?"

"I think so," I answered.

"And don't they use it on vampires?" He continued.

We were all silent.

I ran my hand across the cross. It felt warm, as if heated from the inside. I held it, found that it was only a little bit larger than my hand. On impulse I stuffed it into my jacket pocket. It was a tight fit, but I was able to get the cross in. Then I reached for the wineskin.

"What are you doing?" Michael asked.

"Taking this stuff with us. I just feel safer with it." I looped the strap over my shoulder. "Did you guys find anything else?"

"Nothing," Angie said. "The place is a real mess."

"So what do we do now?" Brand asked.

I looked around. They were all staring at me, expecting an answer. "Do you know where your grandmother was going to meet the police?"

"Yeah," Brand said. "It's only a little ways up the road."

"Why don't we go check just to be sure she isn't still waiting there?" I suggested.

"Well ..." Brand said. "If she is there and she sees me in Grandpa's truck, she'll be pretty mad." He paused. "But I do want to make sure she's alright. She'll understand."

"Then let's go," Angie said.

We made our way out of the house.

» 22 «

"It's just a little bit further on," Brand said.

We had turned off the highway and had been traveling down a gravel road for about ten minutes. The truck's headlights only made a slight glowing dent in the darkness. Trees crowded around us. Little wisps of fog drifted here and there. "I'm sure it is. Just keep your eyes peeled."

I was beginning to feel that familiar cold again. Right down to my bones.

"Is there any heat in this truck?" Michael asked. So I wasn't the only one who was freezing.

Brand cranked on the heater. "It'll take a while for it to warm up. I can't believe how much the temperature has dropped."

The fog was getting thicker. Our lights seemed to be fading, not even close to casting brightness as far as they had before.

We crawled ahead. The truck didn't get any warmer.

"I think that's it, coming up." Brand pointed. "I'm sure of it."

I could see a turn-off ahead that led onto a flat, open area. As we got closer I saw that it was a rest stop in the middle of nowhere. "This is where a lot of the hunters park when they go hunting," Brand explained. We turned off the road. The clearing ended suddenly, surrounded by a wall of trees and underbrush. It was obviously empty.

"Well, she's not here," Brand said. "We must have missed her, somehow." He stepped on the gas, began doing a U-turn.

I saw a glint of metal in the trees as the truck's lights swept the area. "Wait a second," I said.

"What is it?" Brand stepped on the brakes.

"I thought I saw something reflect the lights out there." He backed up and swung the truck the other way.

"There!" I pointed my finger when the light glinted again. "Right there!"

"I see it," Michael said.

Brand pulled straight ahead. A few of the trees were broken and bent over as if something big had been dragged across them. "I can't see anything through all this underbrush. We'll have to take a closer look on foot."

"Go outside?" Angie asked.

"It'll be okay," I said, flicking on my flashlight. "We won't be too far from the truck."

Brand left the Chevy running. We got out and made our way to the underbrush. I ducked and fought my way through thorn trees that poked at me. Whatever was out there was still too far away to see. I could just barely make out a large shape.

"That's weird," Michael said. He stopped for a second, bent over, and rubbed at his ankle.

"What is?" I asked.

"Well you know that bruise I got last night? It's aching like crazy. I can hardly put any weight on it. And my cut hurts too. The farther we get into this bush … the more it hurts."

"Do you want to go back to the truck?" Brand asked.

Michael stood up. "No. I'll be okay. It's not too far away."

We carried on, forcing our way through the underbrush until we came into a clearing. I pointed my light, Angie pointed hers.

I drew in my breath.

It was Althea's truck.

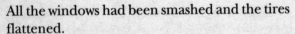

» 23 «

All the windows had been smashed and the tires flattened.

"Grandma!" Brand yelled, and before I could say anything he went running to the truck. I followed, the light from my flashlight bobbing and jumping with each motion. I could barely see where I was going.

I reached the truck a step behind Brand. He yanked open the door and glass rained down onto the ground. "Grandma! Where are you?"

I pointed the light inside the cab, over Brand's shoulder. It was empty. Broken glass was scattered across the seat. Brand backed out, went around the other side yelling.

Angie and Michael joined us. "What happened?" Angie asked.

"I don't know — an accident I guess." All I could see was glass and twisted metal. The door looked bent. Had Brand done that? I shone my light along the side. "Do you remember these dents?" I asked.

"No," Michael answered. "It was in rough shape, but I don't remember anything like that."

"Get a light over here!" Brand yelled. He sounded desperate. We ran around to the other side of the truck, both pointing our flashlights. Brand was down on one knee, examining something. "Closer! Closer!"

I ran up. On the ground in front of Brand was Althea's shawl. Or half of it at least. It had been torn in two. Brand was gripping it tightly. "Whoever did this is going to pay." He stood up, the shawl in his hand. His face was pale and his jaw muscles tight. "Someone's dragged her away."

I pointed my flashlight just past him, illuminating a trail of broken branches and turned up dirt. "You're right … it looks like they went that way."

Brand handed her shawl to me. "I'm going to find her."

"Wait," I said, "we should go back to Grandpa's and call the police. Then we can start looking."

Brand shook his head. "No." He reached out and took the flashlight from Angie's hands. "You three take the truck and head back there. I'm going to look for Grandma." Then he turned on his heel and started running through the trees.

"But we shouldn't split up!" I yelled.

He was already gone. A small blur in the distance, flashlight bobbing like a firefly.

I looked at the other two.

"Now what?" Michael asked.

I shrugged. "Let's hurry back to Grandpa's and phone the RCMP. Then we'll double back here and help him look."

They agreed. We turned and forced our way through the underbrush, heading for the truck. Its lights were a beacon to guide us. A thorn scratched a line across my forehead. When we got closer, I realized something was wrong, there was a sound I couldn't hear. I made it through the last branches into the open.

"Didn't Brand leave the truck running?" I asked.

"I … I can't remember." Angie was silhouetted in the

lights, squinting. "I hope the battery didn't die."

I got in the driver's side, found the keys. They were in the on position. Michael and Angie jumped in the passenger side. I took a deep breath, pushed in the clutch, and turned the key.

Nothing.

I tried again.

Nothing.

"Oh, no," Angie whispered. "This is bad."

"Hurry. Hit the dash or spin the steering wheel or something," Michael suggested. "Maybe it's just some kind of loose wire." I did those things, moving the wheel and twisting the key as hard as I could.

Just when I was about to give up, the motor began to turn. And turn and turn, slower and slower, like it was losing power. "C'mon," Michael said, slamming his fist on the dash.

I thought I could hear a ghost of a sound, like someone yelling in the distance, maybe even calling my name, then the truck roared suddenly and I stomped on the gas a few times. "It started! It started!" I exclaimed.

It took me a moment to find reverse. The gears ground. I pressed the gas too hard and we shot backwards, a cloud of dust filling our headlights. I slammed on the brakes and we skidded in a half circle. When we came to a stop I realized we were on the road, pointing towards the highway.

"Great driving, Sis," Michael said. I didn't know if he was being sarcastic or not.

I found another gear, stepped on the accelerator, and the truck rocketed forward into the mist. "Not so fast," Angie said. "We can hardly see two feet in front of us."

It was true. The fog had grown grayer and thicker. Our light seemed to bounce off it. But I had to hurry. Brand was out there all alone.

And Grandpa and Althea.

"The cops must have been here and not seen her truck," Angie said.

"Probably," I agreed. "It was pretty far in the trees."

"Yeah, but how did it get there?" Michael asked. "She wouldn't have accidentally driven it into the trees."

"Maybe she was trying to hit something," Angie suggested.

"Or it got dragged in there," I added.

"By what? What could drag it in there?" Michael asked.

"The same thing that put the hole in Grandpa's cabin."

We were silent for a moment. No one seemed to want to argue with me.

The fog was clearing a little, so I sped up.

Angie screamed. A moment later I saw why. A figure was on the road in front of us.

The little boy. The ghost boy. Holding out his hands, warning us to stop.

I slammed on the brakes, but it was too late — we were heading right through him. He turned into mist and we came over a small rise into clear air, the truck skidding on gravel.

There in front of us, illuminated for a second, was a half man, half monster, his mouth open in a growl.

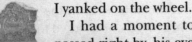I yanked on the wheel.

I had a moment to see him clearly as we passed right by, his eyes huge and glowing, his dirty, lumpy hair blowing in the wind. We were so close he could have reached in the driver window with his enormous arms and yanked me out.

The truck fishtailed past.

The wheel spun, I lost control, and we shot into the ditch and up an embankment, saplings snapping in front of us. It didn't seem like we were going very fast anymore, or perhaps my mind was slowing everything down.

We piled into an old, giant pine tree. I was thrown forward, my head bashed into the steering wheel, and I rolled down to the floor.

Then there was only blackness.

For a few moments I thought I heard voices all around me telling me to wake up, that it was time to move, to go. They sounded so familiar. They gave me the courage to open my eyes.

I couldn't see anything. I heard moaning though. I wasn't sure if it was coming from me or not. I tried to move and found my body wouldn't respond. Had I broken any bones?

Why hadn't I put on my seat belt? I was in too much of a hurry, I had forgotten it.

I realized it wasn't me who was moaning. It was Michael or Angie. They must have been hurt bad. I twisted my head to look but this sent a sharp signal of pain to my brain.

I wasn't going to do that again for awhile. I hoped nothing was wrong with my spine.

There was a noise, a small cracking sound outside the truck.

This was followed by the sound of wrenching metal. Something was trying to yank the passenger door from its hinges. A cold blast of air came in.

"Help me," Angie was whispering. *"Help … me."*

I could hear her sliding on the seat. I tried to move but couldn't. She started to scream, then was suddenly muffled as if a hand had covered her mouth.

I heard a thump.

Then silence.

The crack of snapping twigs was followed by the sound of sniffing. The smell of old graveyard earth — a dark, dank scent, rotten and sweet at the same time — rolled into the truck.

This time Michael moaned, then yelled in panic, *"Hhhhey … let —"*

He fell silent. Something else cracked. Not a twig.

Was it a bone? Michael's neck?

I still couldn't turn my head or move.

The familiar cold had stolen the strength from my limbs.

But not all of the feeling.

Because something rough and strong was wrapping itself around my ankle. It felt like the gnarled roots of a tree in the shape of a hand. The grip grew tighter and tighter so that I almost cried out in pain.

Then it began to pull. I slid towards the other door, helplessly dragged across the floormats. I latched onto the brake pedal with my left hand.

With my right I grabbed the gas pedal.

Now I heard grunting, a wet monstrous roar, as it exerted more strength, trying to get me loose. I held tight, feeling the muscles in my arms and my legs stretching. I heard a popping sound as the vertebrae in my back straightened.

"No. No," I whispered through clenched teeth. *"You can't have me."*

This seemed to anger it. The grip on my ankle doubled, threatening to crush my bones. It roared, pulling so hard that I felt like any moment now I would snap in two.

My fingers started slipping. Bit by bit. I didn't have near enough strength to hold on. Whatever had a hold of me was too strong.

I kicked my free foot in the air, but couldn't hit anything. Then I slid it to the side and propped it against the seat, finding even more leverage.

"You can't have me," I repeated. *"Let me go!"*

Again came the rumbling growling sound, like a dog but larger, wilder. It breathed out. And yanked harder.

My shoe came off, the thing's grip slipped.

I heard a *whomp* as something huge hit the ground. I knew I would only have a second. I let go of the pedals, scrambled onto the seat, and reached out into the cold air to grab the open door.

It wouldn't budge. The door was bent open. There was a blur in my vision to the right of me, moving fast.

Coming straight for me.

I tugged hard, getting my whole body into it. The truck's door screeched and scraped shut with a bang.

A second later the whole truck shook as a heavy weight

plowed into its side. I tried to roll up the window, but realized suddenly the glass was gone.

A giant fist struck the door. The metal bent inwards. I quickly backed away. A second blow bubbled the door, spraying me with bits of metal and glass. I snapped my eyes shut and held up my hands.

When I opened them again I could see two glowing pools of light — eyes peering in at me. A huge, dark, hairy arm the size of a boa constrictor reached in, fingers spread wide. The truck groaned.

I pushed back against the driver's side, tucking my legs under me. I tried to open the door, but the handle wouldn't budge.

The hand came closer, the face pressed in the window. Eyes glowering.

I reached around for something to hit it with. My hand bumped a solid small weight in my jacket pocket.

I unzipped the pocket and grabbed the cross my grandfather had carved.

It felt hot. I held it out in front of me and the cross glowed dull blue. I knew it wasn't moonlight.

The monster paused. He pulled back slightly but not out of the window. It was like he was deciding what to do next.

"Get back!" I hissed, surprised at how solid my voice sounded. "Get out!"

The eyes blinked. Still it didn't move.

"You're Kar, aren't you?" I said. "Kar. You were a man once, weren't you?"

It breathed out, a slow sighing movement. The snakelike pupils went from my face to the cross then back to my face.

"Do you remember?" I asked. "Once you were a man."

The yellow eyes blinked.

"I'm Sarah Asmundson," I said, not sure why. I wanted it to know that I was a person. Maybe somewhere inside him there was still something human. "You have my grandfather … Thursten. You — "

It was the wrong thing to say. The pupils suddenly glowed, his eyes narrowed. With a hiss he pressed against the truck and leaned in, extending his arm to full length.

He grabbed at the cross.

There was a blinding flash of light. A smell of burning flesh. Kar screamed and fell back. I was hit by a shock wave that drove my head into the door.

I saw bright swirling lights.

Then darkness.

25

I opened my eyes, turned my groggy head. I had no idea how long I was out. My skull ached, my ankle, my arms — my whole body felt like a herd of buffalo had stampeded across it twice. The interior of the truck smelled like smoke and burnt flesh. I felt my hair; some of it came away in my hands.

What had happened?

I inhaled and held my breath. Listening. There was nothing. Just silence. I looked, but everywhere was inky darkness. I couldn't see a thing through the windows.

I peeked my head up a little higher and stared out the back. By squinting I could make out a huge lumpy shape moving on two feet. It disappeared into the bushes.

It looked like it was carrying two sacks of potatoes.

Michael and Angie. Kar was taking them away.

I had to do something. I had to.

But what? I scrambled around the truck, searching for the flashlight. It was like one of those nightmares where you need something really bad but it just keeps slipping out of your grasp. It could have gone anywhere when the truck went off the road. Even been thrown out.

My hand felt something hard and round under the seat.

I pulled.

The flashlight.

I pushed the switch forward. No light. Nothing.

I slapped the flashlight in my other hand, a movement I'd seen my father do a hundred times before when he was going out in the night to check the dogs. That moved the batteries around and suddenly the flashlight grew bright, shrinking my pupils.

I pointed it down.

The cross was on the seat. Broken in two.

The wood was still smoldering. I touched it and burnt my hand.

I knew it wouldn't be any help anymore.

I climbed out of the truck. I felt on my back. I still had the wineskin. I had no idea whether it would do me any good.

I took a deep breath and started in the direction I'd last seen Kar. My ankle almost collapsed beneath my weight, but I carried on, pushing into the underbrush, branches slapping at my face. Even in the dull light, his trail was easy to follow. Broken bushes, bent saplings, and huge prints in the soft earth.

I charged on, deeper into the woods, running past trees, tripping over roots. Getting up and running again.

No one's going to find us, I thought. All of us could die out here, lost in the trees.

I should have phoned the police.

A few steps later it dawned on me that they were probably patrolling the area. They'd see the truck all smashed up and suspect that something was going on. Maybe they'd come looking, see Althea's truck too. Just maybe.

I headed on. Twigs cracking below me. The mist grew heavier again, tendrils reaching through the trees. When I looked down, I couldn't even see my feet, it was so thick. I could fall into a pit without knowing it.

But I had to carry on.

The trail was growing harder to follow. There was too much fog. Too much darkness.

A few steps later the flashlight went black.

I stopped, slapped the light against my hand. It wouldn't work. I took out the batteries and put them back in again. No luck.

I gave up and kept moving ahead, slower now, squinting and dodging trees. I gripped the flashlight tight in my hand. It was heavy enough to be a good weapon.

But against what? Kar had bested my grandfather who had a shotgun. Had crushed Hugin. What could I do against him?

Sarah, a voice said inside my head, *stop thinking that way. Just keep going.* I was sure it was my own voice — but why did it sound like Grandma Asmundson? She couldn't be talking to me. Not from heaven.

But a lot of strange things had already happened tonight.

My imagination was getting to me. All I knew was that I had to charge on, no matter what.

A sudden dark flash in my head made me stumble and fall to my knees. I felt claustrophobic suddenly, had an image of darkness, boards being moved, and could hear my brother whispering: *no no no no no.*

I knew what it was. I was feeling the same thing as Michael. He was being shoved in a shallow hole and covered with earth. I could sense him choking, clawing, fighting to keep the dirt from blocking his mouth.

My brother was being buried alive.

Then the image flew away from me and I was left

crouching, feeling sick.

I got up again. Michael needed me. Grandpa. Angie. Althea. They all needed me to keep going.

But how would I find them? I'd lost the trail in the darkness and mist.

I looked up at the moon, a silver face peering through the trees. It wasn't bright enough to light my way.

I couldn't just stand here.

I gathered my courage and started walking in the direction that seemed correct. Looking for any sign that I was going the right way.

After about five minutes I began to panic. I was lost. I wasn't even sure where the road was … ahead of me or behind me. I might have made a circle. I could wander out here for days with no hope of finding anything.

I leaned against a tree. It was hopeless.

Then I looked up.

In the distance a light was glowing.

26

I ran towards it blindly, not caring if I fell or smacked my head against a tree.

It retreated. So I sped up.

I couldn't tell what kind of light it was … a flashlight? A torch? Maybe I should yell.

Just as I opened my mouth to holler, the light disappeared.

I picked up my pace, heading for the last place where I had seen it. Moonlight glinted through the tops of the trees, lighting some of my way. Painting everything white and silver.

I stopped when I heard a noise.

"Help! Help!" It was a small voice. Very far away and familiar.

I took a few steps. Listened.

Nothing.

I moved my left foot ahead.

"Help! Help!"

The cry came from directly in front of me. But there was nothing there. Just a bit of a clearing. A few bushes. Grass.

"Who is it?" I whispered.

No answer.

I moved my right foot.

Even in the moonlight I could see a dark round O in the ground. And I could hear splashing water.

"Hello?" I said.

"Hello! Sarah is that you?" It was Brand's voice. Yelling up from far below me.

"Brand! What happened?" I got down on my hands and knees, careful not to move too far ahead.

"I — I don't know. I was looking for Grandma. My flashlight stopped working and next thing I knew I fell down here — in a well." He paused. "I think someone pushed me though."

"Are you alright?"

"Yes. But — something looked down a few minutes ago, Sarah. It was big. Its head filled the hole. It was an animal I think."

I knew it was worse than an animal. "Can you get out?" I asked.

"I can't climb up. The walls are too slick. I'm treading water right now. Is there a rope or something up there you can toss to me?"

I looked around. "Nothing. How far down are you?" I couldn't see anything but darkness. I heard another splash.

"About thirty feet, I think. It's deep. I can just kind of see you."

"So a tree branch wouldn't work, then?"

"No."

We were quiet a second. "It — " I started, then cleared my throat, " — that thing that looked in at you has Angie and Michael. And Althea too." I paused. "We wrecked the truck."

"The '57 doesn't matter." I heard him breathe in. "Listen Sarah, I'll be okay here. There's a ledge I can hang on to. You … you try and help Angie and Michael and every-one. Come back and get me."

"Are you sure?"

"Yes. Go. I can last for hours down here."

I paused. "Okay. I will. Take care of yourself."

"Just get there!"

Then I was off again. Running. Careful not to fall in the well.

A few hundred feet farther and the light appeared again.

A glowing light. With a tiny figure inside.

I realized what it was.

The boy. The ghost. Showing me the way.

A moment later I saw the cabin.

» 27 «

It was the cabin from my nightmare.

The door was half open, the house lopsided. Wind and rain had hammered on it for years, twisting it into an almost living shape. I knew the boards and logs had soaked up enough evil to stain them black.

Somewhere inside I would find everyone.

Or their bodies.

I had to stop thinking that way. But it had been so long since Grandpa was taken.

What hope was there?

The boy had disappeared. If he had ever even been there.

I swallowed. Somewhere behind me, Brand was treading water, thirty feet below the ground. I needed to hurry if I was going to do anything.

I snuck around the side of the cabin, using the trees as cover. I inched up to the wall and tried to look in the window. The glass was thick and round. It seemed to be made from the bottoms of old, dark, wine bottles. I couldn't see a thing through it.

I crept to the back of the house, looking left and right. I could make out an entrance to a cellar. I went up to it, bent down and listened, but heard nothing. I put my hand to the rope handle. Maybe there was some clue inside.

I couldn't pull. I didn't want to see what was under a cabin as horrendous as this one.

They can't be there, I decided. I released the handle. They can't be.

I went around the other side, found another window. It was even darker than the first one. I crept to the front of the cabin. There was a small porch and a half-open door.

I had to go inside. There was no other choice. I stole along the wall, up to the wooden floorboards. Fresh dirt was scattered in front of the door.

I stepped on the porch and the whole house moaned in protest, as if it knew I was there. I took another step and the board creaked. The wood was so brittle it could hardly carry my weight.

I set my hand on the door, staying to one side, and pushed slowly.

It creaked open.

I peeked around the corner. I couldn't see anything inside but shadows. I listened.

No movement.

I came around the corner, took my first step into the cabin. Nothing.

I went further, boards cracking beneath my feet. Was the cellar under me? Would I fall right through?

I took another step and another, till I was past the door.

My eyes slowly adjusted to this black, black darkness.

I could see a broken table in one corner, a chair. An old bed. All dimly visible.

This would be an awful place to live.

And to die.

I edged ahead. There was dirt piled here and there on the floor. The cabin smelled musty and rotten. Then I stepped again.

My foot caught on something and I fell, headlong, letting go of the flashlight, sucking in air, trying not to scream.

Down, down, down.

But not onto the floor.

I hit a body.

I pushed myself up. Something big and cold and once alive was below me.

I rolled away from it.

Right into another body. Two big pale glassy eyes stared into mine.

I bit my tongue to keep from screaming. I sat up, backed away again.

Then I saw the horns. Just above the eyes. The four legs and hooves.

They were deer.

And cows.

Dead and strewn across the floor. Even in the dark I could see that some of them were half eaten. I heard flies buzzing quietly, back and forth.

There must have been at least six bodies. It was hard to tell because some of them only had the heads left.

Torn apart as if by some wild animal.

I stood in the center of the cabin now. Looking around.

Had the same thing happened to Grandpa? To Michael? Angie?

Nothing seemed to be alive in the room. Maybe that was good.

I stepped over the body of a deer. I squinted my eyes and looked around.

But I couldn't see anything.

Then a glittering caught my attention, a movement in the corner of my eye.

The ghost boy was standing at the other end of the cabin.

28

He looked sad, lost, afraid.

I knew exactly how he felt.

"Bad," he whispered. His mouth kept moving but no words came out.

He stopped, seemed to be crying. His big eyes looking at me.

"I know," I whispered. "It's a bad place. I know, Eric."

His eyes widened when he heard his name. It really was him.

"Are you … trapped here?" I suddenly had an image of Eric still searching for his family in the trees after all this time. He didn't seem to understand my question. He kept blinking his eyes.

"Bad man," he moaned, *"bad man put dirt on me."*

It must have been Kormak, Kar's father. Fifty years ago he had buried this child. Then, how many years later, his son had come to take away my grandfather. What kind of a family were they? Evil ran in their blood.

I imagined Eric spending the last fifty years warning people away from this place. Not wanting the same thing to happen to anyone else. Maybe there was some way I could help him. To release him.

"You will be free," I promised. "Your mother will hold you again … soon."

He was crying now, big watery tears that fell from his face and disappeared before they hit the floor. I wished I could somehow hug him. I didn't dare move closer; he might vanish.

He wiped at his eyes. *"Under boards. Buried. Good. Buried old man."*

My heartbeat skipped. "Do you mean Grandpa?"

This question made Eric point down below him, stomping little feet that made no noise. *"Hurry … fast … buried … bad man coming."*

I stepped towards him.

"Bad man coming," he repeated.

Another step and he vanished.

I went to where he had been standing. Stood there. What did he mean?

A cry came from beneath my feet.

29

It was human sounding. Soft. A moan of pain.
It was so familiar.

"Grandpa?" I asked, getting down on my knees. "Grandpa?"

Another whispering groan.

I felt around, found an edge on one of the boards. I pulled up with all my strength. Slivers bit into my hands, but still I kept working.

Finally, with a creaking protest, the board came up.

I looked down, couldn't see anything but blackness. I yanked up another board.

A sliver of moonlight came through a crack in the roof, lighting up the space in front of me. There was a thin oval, a nose, mouth, closed eyes. An old and wrinkled face. Half buried in the dirt.

"Grandpa!" I exclaimed. "Grandpa!"

I touched his cheek. It was cold, so cold that I feared he was dead.

His eyes opened, slowly. "Sarah," he whispered, his voice gravelly. I realized he probably hadn't had any water for over a day. "Sarah, you're here."

"Yes," I said, "Everything's going to be alright. You're

alive. I knew you would be. I'm going to get you out."

He blinked. "I can't move. I feel like I've been in a freezer for ten years. Now I know what a sirloin steak feels like." He tried to smile, but couldn't.

"Grandpa," I asked, "is it … the man … thing … is it what I think it is?"

He blinked. "Yes. Too much hate inside him to stay dead."

I swallowed. "He — " I said urgently, "Kar has Michael and Sarah and Althea too."

This seemed to wake Grandpa up. "Help me out of here. First close the door."

I went over and pushed the door shut.

"Now what?" I asked when I was standing over him again.

Grandpa blinked. "Listen very carefully. You must — Oh no!"

"What? What?"

"I'm getting … colder." A frightened tone had come into his voice, his words were slurred.

"Colder? What do you mean?"

"C-c-c-older … colder … whenever he gets … close …"

"I'll dig you out. Now."

"No." It seemed to take all of Grandpa's strength to get these words out. "No … time. You must save … the others. Leave … me."

"But …"

There was a rumbling sound outside, like thunder.

"Go," he whispered. "Speak *sofa af nótt*." He seemed to be rambling, not making any sense. "*Sofa … af..nótt.* Go … trust … your blood."

He closed his eyes.

A weight hit the door and it rattled on its hinges.

30

I jumped back against the wall. There was a soft *sst* sound as something sharp and thin poked into my back.

Then I felt a wet warm liquid running down my back.

Blood! I was bleeding.

I felt behind me, discovered that the wineskin I was carrying had been punctured and was leaking water down my back. I had hit an old nail.

The consecrated water! I knew I needed it and here it was pouring out onto the floor.

I pulled the wineskin around to my front, desperately trying to find the hole.

It had been punctured on both sides, was nearly empty.

A second blow hit the door and the top hinge came flying off and tumbled across the floor.

I couldn't just stand there. I leapt over the dead animals and threw all my weight against the door. I picked up a piece of wood and braced it across the frame.

There was breathing outside, an angry tortured sound. Human and animal.

"Blood. Hunnggr. Smell your blood." A harsh raspy whisper.

With a roar, Kar crashed into the door again and the planks snapped inwards.

But the door held.

There was a moment of silence.

I couldn't hear any movement outside. Just the blood pounding in my ears, my heart beating loud as a drum.

But he seemed to be gone.

He couldn't have given up.

I leaned against the door, pressing my ear closer, straining to listen.

A fist came through an inch away from my nose. A hand as big as a shovel, with thick, hairy fingers, reached for me.

I ducked but he caught my hair, started to reel me in.

I pulled back. He had too much hair and was too strong — I couldn't escape.

With a desperate movement I grabbed the wineskin and poured what was left of the water onto his hand, yelling at the same time.

His skin hissed, smoke rose up. He screamed on the other side of the door, let go of my hair, and I fell to the ground.

I could hear him snarling outside the door, stamping and smashing into things. The cabin felt like it would cave in.

Then he ran crazily around, throwing his body against the thick log walls. The windows shattered, dust and wood and shingles fell in on me.

Again he piled himself into the walls like a battering ram.

He howled. But this time it was a retreating cry. Like he was running into the forest, away from the cabin.

31

I listened for what must have been a full minute.

Only silence. A whisper of wind in the trees. Nothing more.

I went back to Grandpa.

"Grandpa!" I whispered, urgently. "Wake up!"

He didn't move. I touched his face. He was even colder. But he stirred slightly, seemed to be breathing.

"I'm going to find the others," I said. "Then I'll be back. I promise."

I turned, went for the door.

But where would they be? Where would he hide them?

I remembered the cellar out behind the house. Of course, the only place.

I lifted the wood from the door, pulled it slowly open, peered out with one eye. The overgrown yard looked empty. The light from the moon had brightened, painting it all with white.

I stepped out, a piece of wood gripped in my hand for a weapon.

I went around the house, slowly.

Nothing. Kar was gone.

I came to the cellar door. It took most of my strength to lift it. Creaking, cracking, moaning in protest it came up. The hinges squealing like they hadn't been used in years. I let it drop.

The light of the moon shone over the first three earthen steps.

I started down, my wood in front of me like a sword. It felt flimsy and small. I knew it wouldn't help me in the slightest.

But just holding it made me feel better.

After a few steps I was covered with ebony darkness. I pushed on, the stairs seemed to go quite deep. It was cold in here. The cold of December still seeping out of the earth.

I could make out a small cramped room stuffed with old rotten potato sacks. Two support poles held the floor up. This seemed to cover only half the bottom of the house.

A step later I heard a small noise. A whisper of breath.

I tightened my grip.

But there was more than one person breathing. There were two, then three. I looked down.

Only inches from where I was walking were the faces of Michael and Angie, buried in the dirt, a newly made mound over top of them. A foot or two away was Althea.

All with their eyes closed.

I bent down.

Michael's cheek was igloo cold and covered with small cuts. Had he been dragged on the ground all the way here?

Angie was freezing too and one eye seemed bruised.

Althea had lost her patch. Her blind eye stared whitely at me, her good eye closed.

None of them were awake. When I spoke, no one moved.

I started digging Michael out. The dirt was soft and I found it easy. Within a minute he was free. It took a huge

effort to pull him out of the hole.

Through it all he stayed sleeping.

I worked on Angie next, quickly unearthing her body. When I was finished I pulled her over beside Michael.

I started on Althea. About halfway through I heard a creaking noise above me. A heavy inhalation of air.

I turned to see the moonlight blocked by a huge shape coming down the stairs one slow step at a time. He brushed against the walls with his shoulders, hands out.

Then finally I saw his eyes. Cold, yellow, pitiless — they had changed. There was nothing human in them anymore, no emotions but anger and hunger. He stared right at me through the darkness. His elongated face was twisted into a grimace.

He slouched ahead, unblinking. He stopped to sniff at Michael and Angie.

I backed up, farther, farther.

Then I hit the earth wall.

Kar trudged towards me, his breath rattling in his throat. His hands out. His mouth moved in a chewing motion and I knew he could no longer speak. All he had was a lust for my blood.

Saliva dripped from the edge of his thick lips to the floor below.

I threw the piece of wood at him. It bounced off, harmlessly. He didn't even blink.

His form filled the cellar. He stepped over Althea. Lumbered closer and closer to me. Both his hands were out like huge claws, opening and closing.

I could see strangely shaped muscles bulging and flexing. He could tear me apart in an instant. Turn me to jelly.

He reached out. I put up my arms to ward him off. But still he pressed in on me, his hands touching me. They were cold and covered with earth, slime, and blood.

He forced me harder against the wall, squeezing now, his grip inescapable. His face was closer to mine. I could feel his breath — a cold, harsh wind. His deformed body smelled of rotting flesh.

My ribs felt like they would give. He was going to crush me against the wall.

His face leaned closer in. I saw his eyes, the color of a harvest moon, glowing with huge pitiless pupils. *"Blood ... "* he whispered, his words slurred through his thick, gray lips. Spit spattered my face. *"Blood of ... Asmundson ... must bleed."*

I could see yellow, thick, grainy teeth in his mouth. Sharp.

I closed my eyes. Felt myself curl into a ball, suffocating under his weight.

I would be dead in a moment.

This was the end.

One of these breaths, now so hard to breathe, would be my last.

I surrendered. Waiting. There was nothing I could do.

Then I felt a stirring. Deep inside me. A swirling. Of hope. Of the past. A place I had only visited in my dreams.

An old ancient space inside my fourteen-year-old body. Echoing with voices.

Sarah. Sarah. Sarah.

For a second I felt all of my ancestors, back for a thousand years, in my blood, my heart, my spirit — urging me on. My grandmother, my great-grandfather, even Grettir the Strong were all there. I felt their power added to mine. They were telling me to breathe, reminding me who I was, lending me their strength, their knowledge. I inhaled and they seemed to cheer.

Sarah Asmundson. Sarah.

I set my legs. Then I pushed. Hard.

It was like lifting the weight of a truck, a boulder, a mountain. And still I used this new strength, lifting higher and higher.

Kar made a confused, almost startled, noise. He tried to squeeze me tighter, to fight back. He succeeded in pushing me down a little.

I felt a rush of strength and gave one final heave. Kar suddenly flew backwards, crashed onto the floor, and rolled into one of the support poles. It cracked. A small clump of dirt and pieces of wood fell from the roof, covering him.

He lay there on his back, waving his arms and twisting his neck, looking for me. He was like a beetle that couldn't right itself.

He screamed.

The voices, my ancestors, were gone.

Just me. Alone.

I knew I had to act quickly.

I stood up, rising to my full height, and came towards Kar. My feet were steady.

Kar turned to me. His yellow eyes blinked. His face seemed confused and angry. He tried to move his arms, to reach towards me, but his hands fell uselessly at his side. He opened and closed his fingers like claws.

He tried to scream again, but all that emerged was a hissing of air.

He seemed broken. Whatever gave him power was dying bit by bit.

But would it come back? I didn't know how long I had.

I stood right above Kar, looking down. He bared his teeth, yellow sharp spikes. I knew he would tear open my throat if he could reach me.

I remembered what Grandpa had said. The words. Icelandic words. They came to me as natural as English. *"Sofa af nótt."* I spoke slowly, soothingly. He glared at me.

I knelt next to Kar. This time I almost sang the words — a lullaby. His eyelids slid closed. Then they opened and stared at me, anger making them glow red.

Was he waking up?

Didn't Grandpa say something about them cursing people? With their last bit of strength. A curse that lasted a lifetime.

"Sofa af nótt," I whispered. "Sleep. *Sofa af nótt."* His eyes held mine and I felt a dark emotion entering my thoughts, my spirit.

His curse.

He moved his lips, trying to mouth something.

"Sofa af nótt," I repeated, desperately.

There was a final flare of anger in his eyes. I felt a stabbing pain in the back of my head. My heart stopped.

Then nothing.

His eyelids slid together.

32

He stayed still.

Satisfied, I turned to the others. Althea was getting up, so were Michael and Angie, rubbing their heads.

"What happened?" Michael whispered. "I feel like I've been hit by a bulldozer. Where are we?" He turned to me. "Oh … Sarah, I had the weirdest dream … we crashed the truck and then I was dragged upside down through — "

"Quickly!" I hissed. "Get out of here!"

Michael blinked. Angie stared at me.

Only Althea seemed to understand. "She's right, get up, get out, now!"

With her voice added to mine, they listened. We stumbled up the stairs. Out into the open air.

"Where are — " Angie started.

"C'mon, you've got to help me!" Then I ran around the front of the cabin. "In here!"

They followed me inside. I started tearing at the boards in the floor, madly throwing them behind me.

"Hey watch it!" Michael said. Then he paused. "Grandpa! That's Grandpa!" He pitched in and Angie helped too.

Grandpa opened his eyes a moment later, stared up at

me. He couldn't speak but he smiled.

It took all of us working together to drag him out of the cabin. We stopped when we were about a hundred feet away.

Then we sat there catching our breath.

Suddenly the cabin started to moan, to pitch and twist like a gale of wind had hit it. And with a final crash it collapsed in on itself, imploding, falling and falling down so that not a board was standing.

We stared at the dust, the wreckage.

"Someone's going to have to explain a few things to me," Angie said.

Grandpa looked right at me. "I have a feeling that a lot of this won't be easily explained."

I felt tired, all my strength was leaving me. Something brushed my shoulder and my heart leapt.

I turned to catch a glimpse of glowing light with a figure inside. A little boy smiled at me, then flew upwards. He seemed to be going towards the stars.

"Goodbye, Eric," I whispered.

With my last bit of strength I limped to the house. It took me a moment to find two good-sized planks.

I placed them across each other in the form of a cross.

33

We didn't forget about Brand. We tied our belts and clothes together and lowered our makeshift rope down and pulled him out. Then we walked through the trees silently.

The police found us on the road and after wrapping us with blankets and asking us a hundred and one questions, they took us back to Althea's.

My father and mother arrived the following day. Over the next few days the police returned and asked more questions. I explained to them what I could, left out what I knew they wouldn't understand. They looked through the wreckage of the cabin.

They never found Kar's body. Only old, partly disintegrated bones. They didn't know what kind of animal they were from. They were too big to be a bear or a human.

I wanted to get home. It would take me a lifetime to understand all this.

When we left, Grandpa gave me a big, long hug. "You're made of good stuff," he said. I squeezed him hard, then we were in the rented car on our way to the airport at Winnipeg. I felt older already. Maybe it had changed me.

We went into Gimli and I told my parents to stop at the

Ye Ol' Ice Cream Shoppe. Brand was at the front counter. He came out and stood in front of me.

"Going?" he asked.

"Yes," I said. I glanced up at him and he smiled. He was so handsome that I almost forgot what I wanted to say. "I — I can't stay long. I just wanted to tell you … well … I had fun. Except for Grandpa getting kidnapped and all that stuff." I paused. The next part would be the hardest to get out. "I'm kind of hoping you'll write to me."

"Of course!" His smile got even bigger. "Will you come back next summer? We could go tubing!"

"I wouldn't miss it for the world." I hugged him and gave him a piece of paper with my address on it.

When I got to the door, I turned back. "Brand, do me a favor till next time we see each other … don't fall down any holes, okay? You might meet a rabbit you don't like."

He still smiled, though he looked at me like I was crazy.

I winked. "I'll tell you what it means next summer."

More books for young readers from Orca Book Publishers

COUGAR COVE Julie Lawson
1-55143-072-X; $7.95 (cdn), $6.95 (us); ages 8 to 11

THE FIRST TIME, VOLUME 1 Charles Montpetit, ed.
1-55143-037-1; $7.95 (cdn), $6.95 (us); all ages

THE FIRST TIME, VOLUME 2 Charles Montpetit, ed.
1-55143-039-8; $7.95 (cdn), $6.95 (us); all ages

A FLY NAMED ALFRED Don Trembath
1-55143-083-5; $7.95 (cdn), $6.95 (us); ages 12 to 16

A LIGHT IN THE DUNES martha attema
1-55143-085-1; $7.95 (cdn), $6.95 (us); ages 11 to 14

SKATEWAY TO FREEDOM Ann Alma
0-920501-89-3; $6.95 (cdn), $5.95 (us); ages 7 to 10

SOMETHING WEIRD IS GOING ON Christie Harris
1-55143-022-3; $6.95 (cdn), $5.95 (us); ages 8 to 11

SUMMER OF MADNESS Marion Crook
1-55143-041-X; $7.95 (cdn), $6.95 (us)

THREE AGAINST TIME Margaret Taylor
1-55143-067-3; $7.95 (cdn), $6.95 (us); ages 8 to 12

A TIME TO CHOOSE martha attema
1-55143-045-2; $7.95 (cdn), $6.95 (us); ages 11 to 14

THE TUESDAY CAFE Don Trembath
1-55143-074-6; $7.95 (cdn), $6.95 (us); ages 12 to 16

*For a complete list of books available through Orca Book Publishers,
please call 1-800-210-5277.*